BY GEORGE R. R. MARTIN

A Song of Ice and Fire

Book One: A Game of Thrones
Book Two: A Clash of Kings
Book Three: A Storm of Swords
Book Four: A Feast for Crows
Book Five: A Dance with Dragons
The World of Ice & Fire:
*   The Untold History of Westeros*
*   and the Game of Thrones*

Dying of the Light
Windhaven (with Lisa Tuttle)
Fevre Dream
The Armageddon Rag
Dead Man's Hand (with
    John J. Miller)

Short Story Collections

Dreamsongs: Volume I
Dreamsongs: Volume II
A Song for Lya and Other Stories
Songs of Stars and Shadows
Sandkings
Songs the Dead Men Sing
Nightflyers
Tuf Voyaging
Portraits of His Children
Quartet

Edited by
George R. R. Martin

New Voices in Science Fiction,
*   Volumes 1-4*
The Science Fiction Weight Loss
*   Book* (with Isaac Asimov and
    Martin Harry Greenberg)
The John W. Campbell Awards,
*   Volume 5*
Night Visions 3
Wild Cards I-XXII

Co-edited with Gardner Dozois

Warriors I-III
Songs of the Dying Earth
Down These Strange Streets
Old Mars
Dangerous Women
Rogues
Old Venus
The Book of Swords

NIGHTFLYERS

NIGHTFLYERS

The Illustrated Edition

GEORGE R. R. MARTIN

Bantam Books
New York

2018 Bantam Books Trade Paperback Edition

Copyright © 1980, 1981 by George R. R. Martin
Text illustrations and endpapers copyright © 2018 by David Palumbo

Published in the United States by Bantam Books,
an imprint of Random House,
a division of Penguin Random House LLC, New York.

BANTAM BOOKS and the HOUSE colophon are registered trademarks
of Penguin Random House LLC.

Originally published in hardcover in the United States by
Bantam Books, an imprint of Random House,
a division of Penguin Random House LLC, in 2018.

From *Binary Star 5* (Dell, 1981). A shorter version of this story
originally appeared in *Analog,* April 1980, copyright © 1980 by
the Condé Nast Publications, Inc. Published as part of
Dreamsongs: Volume I (Bantam, 2007).

LIBRARY OF CONGRESS CATALOGING-IN-PUBLICATION DATA

Names: Martin, George R. R., author.
Title: Nightflyers / George R. R. Martin.
Description: Illustrated edition. | New York : Bantam, 2018.
Identifiers: LCCN 2018005083 | ISBN 9780525620891 (trade
paperback) | ISBN 9780525619697 (ebook)
Subjects: LCSH: Space ships—Fiction. | Murder—Fiction. | BISAC:
FICTION / Horror. | GSAFD: Science fiction. | Horror fiction.
Classification: LCC PS3563.A7239 N54 2018 | DDC 813/.54—dc23
LC record available at https://lccn.loc.gov/2018005083

Printed in the United States of America on acid-free paper

randomhousebooks.com

2 4 6 8 9 7 5 3 1

Book design by Virginia Norey

to Gardner Dozois
"Manatees!"

NIGHTFLYERS

WHEN JESUS OF NAZARETH HUNG DYING on his cross, the *volcryn* passed within a year of his agony, headed outward.

When the Fire Wars raged on Earth, the *volcryn* sailed near Old Poseidon, where the seas were still unnamed and unfished. By the time the stardrive had transformed the Federated Nations of Earth into the Federal Empire, the *volcryn* had moved into the fringes of Hrangan space. The Hrangans never knew it. Like us they were children of the small bright worlds that circled their scattered suns, with little interest and less knowledge of the things that moved in the gulfs between.

War flamed for a thousand years and the *volcryn* passed through it, unknowing and untouched, safe in a place where no fires could ever burn. Afterwards, the Federal Empire was shattered and gone, and the Hrangans vanished in the dark of the Collapse, but it was no darker for the *volcryn*.

When Kleronomas took his survey ship out from Avalon, the *volcryn* came within ten light-years of him. Kleronomas found many things, but he did not find the *volcryn*. Not then and not on his return to Avalon, a lifetime later.

When I was a child of three, Kleronomas was dust, as distant and dead as Jesus of Nazareth, and the *volcryn* passed close to Daronne. That season all the Crey sensitives grew strange and sat staring at the stars with luminous, flickering eyes.

When I was grown, the *volcryn* had sailed beyond Tara, past the range of even the Crey, still heading outward.

And now I am old and growing older and the *volcryn* will soon pierce the Tempter's Veil where it hangs like a black mist between the stars. And we follow, we follow. Through the dark gulfs where no one goes, through the emptiness, through the silence that goes on and on, my *Nightflyer* and I give chase.

They made their way slowly down the length of the transparent tube that linked the orbital docks to the waiting starship ahead, pulling themselves hand over hand through weightlessness.

Melantha Jhirl, the only one among them who did not seem clumsy and ill at ease in free fall, paused briefly to look at the dappled globe of Avalon below, a stately vastness in jade and amber. She smiled and moved swiftly down the tube, passing her companions with an easy grace. They had boarded starships before, all of them, but never like this. Most ships docked flush against the station, but the craft that Karoly d'Branin had chartered for his mission was too large, and too singular in design. It loomed ahead; three small eggs side by side, two larger spheres beneath and at right angles, the cylinder of the driveroom between, lengths of tube connecting it all. The ship was white and austere.

Melantha Jhirl was the first one through the airlock. The others straggled up one by one until they had all boarded; five women and four men, each an Academy scholar, their backgrounds as diverse as their fields of study. The frail young telepath, Thale Lasamer, was the last to enter. He glanced about nervously as the others chatted and waited for the entry procedure to be completed. "We're being watched," he said.

The outer door was closed behind them, the tube had fallen away; now the inner door slid open. "Welcome to my *Nightflyer*," said a mellow voice from within.

But there was no one there.

Melantha Jhirl stepped into the corridor. "Hello," she said, looking about quizzically. Karoly d'Branin followed her.

"Hello," the mellow voice replied. It was coming from a communicator grille beneath a darkened viewscreen. "This is Royd Eris, master of the *Nightflyer*. I'm pleased to see you again, Karoly, and pleased to welcome the rest of you."

"Where are you?" someone demanded.

"In my quarters, which occupy half of this life-support sphere," the voice of Royd Eris replied amiably. "The other half is comprised of a lounge-library-kitchen, two sanitary stations, one double cabin, and a rather small single. The rest of you will have to rig sleepwebs in the cargo spheres, I'm afraid. The *Nightflyer* was designed as a trader, not a passenger vessel. However, I've opened all the appropriate passageways and locks, so the holds have air and heat and water. I thought you'd find it more comfortable that way. Your equipment and computer system have been stowed in the holds, but there is still plenty of space, I assure you. I suggest you settle in, and then meet in the lounge for a meal."

"Will you join us?" asked the psipsych, a querulous hatchet-faced woman named Agatha Marij-Black.

"In a fashion," Royd Eris said, "in a fashion."

* * *

The ghost appeared at the banquet.

They found the lounge easily enough, after they had rigged their sleepwebs and arranged their personal belongings around their sleeping quarters. It was the largest room in this section of the ship. One end of it was a fully equipped kitchen, well stocked with provisions. The opposite end offered several comfortable chairs, two readers, a holotank, and a wall of books and tapes and crystal chips. In the center was a long table with places set for ten.

A light meal was hot and waiting. The academicians helped themselves and took seats at the table, laughing and talking to one another, more at ease now than when they had boarded.

The ship's gravity grid was on, which went a long way towards making them more comfortable; the queasy awkwardness of their weightless transit was soon forgotten.

Finally all the seats were occupied except for one at the head of the table.

The ghost materialized there.

All conversation stopped.

"Hello," said the spectre, the bright shade of a lithe, pale-eyed young man with white hair. He was dressed in clothing twenty years out-of-date; a loose blue pastel shirt that ballooned at his wrists, clinging white trousers with built-in boots. They could see through him, and his own eyes did not see them at all.

"A hologram," said Alys Northwind, the short, stout xenotech.

"Royd, Royd, I do not understand," said Karoly d'Branin, staring at the ghost. "What is this? Why do you send us a projection? Will you not join us in person?"

The ghost smiled faintly and lifted an arm. "My quarters are on the other side of that wall," he said. "I'm afraid there is no door or lock between the two halves of the sphere. I spend most of my time by myself, and I value my privacy. I hope you will all understand and respect my wishes. I will be a gracious host nonetheless. Here in the lounge my projection can join you. Elsewhere, if you have anything you need, if you want to talk to me, just use a communicator. Now, please resume your meal, and your conversations. I'll gladly listen. It's been a long time since I had passengers."

They tried. But the ghost at the head of the table cast a long shadow, and the meal was strained and hurried.

* * *

From the hour the *Nightflyer* slipped into stardrive, Royd Eris watched his passengers.

Within a few days most of the academicians had grown accustomed to the disembodied voice from the communicators and the holographic spectre in the lounge, but only Melantha Jhirl and Karoly d'Branin ever seemed really comfortable in his presence. The others would have been even more uncomfortable if they had known that Royd was always with them. Always and everywhere, he watched. Even in the sanitary stations, Royd had eyes and ears.

He watched them work, eat, sleep, copulate; he listened untiringly to their talk. Within a week he knew them, all nine, and had begun to ferret out their tawdry little secrets.

The cyberneticist, Lommie Thorne, talked to her computers and seemed to prefer their company to that of humans. She was bright and quick, with a mobile, expressive face and a small, hard boyish body; most of the others found her attractive, but she did not like to be touched. She sexed only once, with Melantha Jhirl. Lommie Thorne wore shirts of softly woven metal, and had an implant in her left wrist that let her interface directly with her computers.

The xenobiologist, Rojan Christopheris, was a surly,

argumentative man, a cynic whose contempt for his colleagues was barely kept in check, a solitary drinker. He was tall and stooped and ugly.

The two linguists, Dannel and Lindran, were lovers in public, constantly holding hands and supporting each other. In private they quarreled bitterly. Lindran had a mordant wit and liked to wound Dannel where it hurt the most, with jokes about his professional competence. They sexed often, both of them, but not with each other.

Agatha Marij-Black, the psipsych, was a hypochondriac given to black depressions, which worsened in the close confines of the *Nightflyer.*

Xenotech Alys Northwind ate constantly and never washed. Her stubby fingernails were always caked with black dirt, and she wore the same jumpsuit for the first two weeks of the voyage, taking it off only for sex, and then only briefly.

Telepath Thale Lasamer was nervous and temperamental, afraid of everyone around him, yet given to bouts of arrogance in which he taunted his companions with thoughts he had snatched from their minds.

Royd Eris watched them all, studied them, lived with them and through them. He neglected none, not even the ones he found the most distasteful. But by the time the *Nightflyer* had been lost in the roiling flux of stardrive for two weeks, two of his riders had come to engage the bulk of his attention.

"Most of all, I want to know the why of them," Karoly d'Branin told him one false night the second week out from Avalon.

Royd's luminescent ghost sat close to d'Branin in the darkened lounge, watching him drink bittersweet chocolate. The others were all asleep. Night and day are meaningless on a starship, but the *Nightflyer* kept the usual cycles and most of the passengers followed them. Old d'Branin, administrator, generalist, and mission leader, was the exception; he kept his own hours, preferred work to sleep, and liked nothing better than to talk about his pet obsession, the *volcryn* he hunted.

"The *if* of them is important as well, Karoly," Royd answered. "Can you truly be certain these aliens of yours exist?"

"*I* can be certain," Karoly d'Branin said, with a broad wink. He was a compact man, short and slender, iron gray hair carefully styled and his tunic almost fussily neat, but the expansiveness of his gestures and the giddy enthusiasms to which he was prone belied his sober appearance. "That is enough. If everyone else were certain as well, we would have a fleet of research ships instead of your little *Nightflyer*." He sipped at his chocolate and sighed with satisfaction. "Do you know the Nor T'alush, Royd?"

The name was strange, but it took Royd only a moment to consult his library computer. "An alien race on the other side of human space, past the Fyndii worlds and the Damoosh. Possibly legendary."

D'Branin chuckled. "No, no, no! Your library is out-of-date, my friend, you must supplement it the next time you visit Avalon. Not legends, no, real enough, though far away. We have little information about the Nor T'alush, but we are sure they exist, though you and I may never meet one. They were the start of it all."

"Tell me," Royd said. "I am interested in your work, Karoly."

"I was coding some information into the Academy computers, a packet newly arrived from Dam Tullian after twenty standard years in transit. Part of it was Nor T'alush folklore. I had no idea how long that had taken to get to Dam Tullian, or by what route it had come, but it did not matter—folklore is timeless anyway, and this was fascinating material. Did you know that my first degree was in xenomythology?"

"I did not. Please continue."

"The *volcryn* story was among the Nor T'alush myths.

It awed me; a race of sentients moving out from some mysterious origin in the core of the galaxy, sailing towards the galactic edge and, it was alleged, eventually bound for intergalactic space itself, meanwhile always keeping to the interstellar depths, no planetfalls, seldom coming within a light-year of a star." D'Branin's gray eyes sparkled, and as he spoke his hands swept enthusiastically to either side, as if they could encompass the galaxy. "And doing it all *without a stardrive,* Royd, that is the real wonder! Doing it in ships moving only a fraction of the speed of light! That was the detail that obsessed me! How different they must be, my *volcryn*—wise and patient, long-lived and long-viewed, with none of the terrible haste and passion that consumes the lesser races. Think how *old* they must be, those *volcryn* ships!"

"Old," Royd agreed. "Karoly, you said ships. More than one?"

"Oh, yes," d'Branin said. "According to the Nor T'alush, one or two appeared first, on the innermost edges of their trading sphere, but others followed. Hundreds of them, each solitary, moving by itself, bound outward, always outward. The direction was always the same. For fifteen thousand standard years they moved among the Nor T'alush stars, and then they began to pass out from among them. The myth said that the last *volcryn* ship was gone three thousand years ago."

"Eighteen thousand years," Royd said, adding, "Are the Nor T'alush that old?"

"Not as star-travelers, no," d'Branin said, smiling. "According to their own histories, the Nor T'alush have only been civilized for about half that long. That bothered me for a while. It seemed to make the *volcryn* story clearly a legend. A wonderful legend, true, but nothing more.

"Ultimately, however, I could not let it alone. In my spare time I investigated, cross-checking with other alien cosmologies to see whether this particular myth was shared by any races other than the Nor T'alush. I thought perhaps I could get a thesis out of it. It seemed a fruitful line of inquiry.

"I was startled by what I found. Nothing from the Hrangans, or the Hrangan slave races, but that made sense, you see. Since they were *out* from human space, the *volcryn* would not reach them until after they had passed through our own sphere. When I looked *in,* however, the *volcryn* story was everywhere." D'Branin leaned forward eagerly. "Ah, Royd, the stories, the *stories!*"

"Tell me," Royd said.

"The Fyndii call them *iy-wivii,* which translates to

something like void-horde or dark-horde. Each Fyndii horde tells the same story, only the mindmutes disbelieve. The ships are said to be vast, much larger than any known in their history or ours. Warships, they say. There is a story of a lost Fyndii horde, three hundred ships under *rala-fyn,* all destroyed utterly when they encountered an *iy-wivii.* This was many thousands of years ago, of course, so the details are unclear.

"The Damoosh have a different story, but they accept it as literal truth—and the Damoosh, you know, are the oldest race we've yet encountered. The people of the gulf, they call my *volcryn.* Lovely stories, Royd, lovely! Ships like great dark cities, still and silent, moving at a slower pace than the universe around them. Damoosh legends say the *volcryn* are refugees from some unimaginable war deep in the core of the galaxy, at the very beginning of time. They abandoned the worlds and stars on which they had evolved, sought true peace in the emptiness between.

"The gethsoids of Aath have a similar story, but in their tale that war destroyed all life in our galaxy, and the *volcryn* are gods of a sort, reseeding the worlds as they pass. Other races see them as god's messengers, or shadows out of hell warning us all to flee some terror soon to emerge from the core."

"Your stories contradict each other, Karoly."

"Yes, yes, of course, but they all agree on the essentials—the *volcryn,* sailing out, passing through our short-lived empires and transient glories in their ancient eternal sublight ships. *That* is what matters! The rest is frippery, ornamentation; we will soon know the truth of it. I checked what little was known about the races said to flourish farther in still, beyond even the Nor T'alush—civilizations and peoples half legendary themselves, like the Dan'lai and the ullish and the Rohenna'kh—and where I could find anything at all, I found the *volcryn* story once again."

"The legend of the legends," Royd suggested. The spectre's wide mouth turned up in a smile.

"Exactly, exactly," d'Branin agreed. "At that point, I called in the experts, specialists from the Institute for the Study of Non-Human Intelligence. We researched for two years. It was all there, in the libraries and memories and matrices of the Academy. No one had ever looked before, or bothered to put it together.

"The *volcryn* have been moving through the manrealm for most of human history, since before the dawn of spaceflight. While we twist the fabric of space itself to cheat relativity, they have been sailing their great ships right through the heart of our alleged civilization, past our most populous worlds, at stately, slow sublight speeds, bound for the Fringe and the dark between the galaxies. Marvelous, Royd, marvelous!"

"Marvelous!" Royd agreed.

Karoly d'Branin drained his chocolate cup with a swig, and reached out to catch Royd's arm, but his hand passed through empty light. He seemed disconcerted for a moment, before he began to laugh at himself. "Ah, my *volcryn*. I grow overenthused, Royd. I am so close now. They have preyed on my mind for a dozen years, and within the month I will have them, will behold their splendor with my own weary eyes. Then, then, if only I can open communication, if only my people can reach ones so great and strange as they, so different from us—I have hopes, Royd, hopes that at last I will know the why of it!"

The ghost of Royd Eris smiled for him, and looked on through calm transparent eyes.

Passengers soon grow restless on a starship under drive, sooner on one as small and spare as the *Nightflyer*. Late in the second week, the speculation began in deadly earnest.

"Who is this Royd Eris, really?" the xenobiologist,

Rojan Christopheris, complained one night when four of them were playing cards. "Why doesn't he come out? What's the purpose of keeping himself sealed off from the rest of us?"

"Ask him," suggested Dannel, the male linguist.

"What if he's a criminal of some sort?" Christopheris said. "Do we know anything about him? No, of course not. D'Branin engaged him, and d'Branin is a senile old fool, we all know that."

"It's your play," Lommie Thorne said.

Christopheris snapped down a card. "Setback," he declared, "you'll have to draw again." He grinned. "As for this Eris, who knows that he isn't planning to kill us all."

"For our vast wealth, no doubt," said Lindran, the female linguist. She played a card on top of the one Christopheris had laid down. "Ricochet," she called softly. She smiled. So did Royd Eris, watching.

Melantha Jhirl was good to watch.

Young, healthy, active, Melantha Jhirl had a vibrancy about her the others could not match. She was big in every way; a head taller than anyone else on board, large-framed, large-breasted, long-legged, strong, muscles moving fluidly beneath shiny coal-black skin. Her appetites were big as well. She ate twice as much as any of her colleagues, drank heavily without ever seeming drunk, exercised for hours every day on equipment she had brought with her and set up in one of the cargo holds. By the third week out she had sexed with all four of the men on board and two of the other women. Even in bed she was always active, exhausting most of her partners. Royd watched her with consuming interest.

"I am an improved model," she told him once as she worked out on her parallel bars, sweat glistening on her bare skin, her long black hair confined in a net.

"Improved?" Royd said. He could not send his projection down to the holds, but Melantha had summoned him with the communicator to talk while she exercised, not knowing he would have been there anyway.

She paused in her routine, holding her body straight and aloft with the strength of her arms and her back. "Altered, captain," she said. She had taken to calling him captain. "Born on Prometheus among the elite, child of two genetic wizards. Improved, captain. I require twice the energy you do, but I use it all. A more efficient metabolism, a stronger and more durable body, an expected life span half again the normal human's. My people have made some terrible mistakes when they try to radically redesign humanity, but the small improvements they do well."

She resumed her exercises, moving quickly and easily, silent until she had finished. When she was done, she vaulted away from the bars and stood breathing heavily for a moment, then crossed her arms and cocked her head and grinned. "Now you know my life story, captain," she said. She pulled off the net to shake free her hair.

"Surely there is more," said the voice from the communicator.

Melantha Jhirl laughed. "Surely," she said. "Do you want to hear about my defection to Avalon, the whys and wherefores of it, the trouble it caused my family on Prometheus? Or are you more interested in my extraordinary work in cultural xenology? Do you want to hear about that?"

"Perhaps some other time," Royd said politely. "What is that crystal you wear?"

It hung between her breasts ordinarily; she had removed it when she stripped for her exercises. She picked it up again and slipped it over her head; a small green gem laced with traceries of black, on a silver chain. When it touched her Melantha closed her eyes briefly, then opened them again, grinning. "It's alive," she said.

"Haven't you ever seen one? A whisperjewel, captain. Resonant crystal, etched psionically to hold a memory, a sensation. The touch brings it back, for a time."

"I am familiar with the principle," Royd said, "but not this use. Yours contains some treasured memory, then? Of your family, perhaps?"

Melantha Jhirl snatched up a towel and began to dry the sweat from her body. "Mine contains the sensations of a particularly satisfying session in bed, captain. It arouses me. Or it did. Whisperjewels fade in time, and this isn't as potent as it once was. But sometimes— often when I've come from lovemaking or strenuous exercise—it comes alive on me again, like it did just then."

"Oh," said Royd's voice. "It has made you aroused, then? Are you going off to copulate now?"

Melantha grinned. "I know what part of my life you want to hear about, captain—my tumultuous and passionate love life. Well, you won't have it. Not until I hear your life story, anyway. Among my modest attributes is an insatiable curiosity. Who are you, captain? Really?"

"One as improved as you," Royd replied, "should certainly be able to guess."

Melantha laughed, and tossed her towel at the communicator grille.

* * *

Lommie Thorne spent most of her days in the cargo hold they had designated as the computer room, setting up the system they would use to analyze the *volcryn*. As often as not, the xenotech Alys Northwind came with her to lend a hand. The cyberneticist whistled as she worked; Northwind obeyed her orders in a sullen silence. Occasionally they talked.

"Eris isn't human," Lommie Thorne said one day, as she supervised the installation of a display viewscreen.

Alys Northwind grunted. "What?" A frown broke across her square, flat features. Christopheris and his talk had made her nervous about Eris. She clicked another component into position, and turned.

"He talks to us, but he can't be seen," the cyberneticist said. "This ship is uncrewed, seemingly all automated except for him. Why not entirely automated, then? I'd wager this Royd Eris is a fairly sophisticated computer system, perhaps a genuine Artificial Intelligence. Even a modest program can carry on a blind conversation indistinguishable from a human's. This one could fool you, I'd bet, once it's up and running."

The xenotech grunted and turned back to her work. "Why fake being human, then?"

"Because," said Lommie Thorne, "most legal systems

give AIs no rights. A ship can't own itself, even on Avalon. The *Nightflyer* is probably afraid of being seized and disconnected." She whistled. "Death, Alys; the end of self-awareness and conscious thought."

"I work with machines every day," Alys Northwind said stubbornly. "Turn them off, turn them on, makes no difference. They don't mind. Why should this machine care?"

Lommie Thorne smiled. "A computer is different, Alys," she said. "Mind, thought, life, the big systems have all of that." Her right hand curled around her left wrist, and her thumb began idly rubbing the nubs of her implant. "Sensation, too. I know. No one wants the end of sensation. They are not so different from you and I, really."

The xenotech glanced back and shook her head. "Really," she repeated, in a flat, disbelieving voice.

Royd Eris listened and watched, unsmiling.

Thale Lasamer was a frail young thing; nervous, sensitive, with limp flaxen hair that fell to his shoulders, and watery blue eyes. Normally he dressed like a peacock, favoring the lacy V-necked shirts and codpieces that were still the fashion among the lower classes of his homeworld. But on the day he sought out Karoly d'Branin in his cramped, private cabin, Lasamer was dressed almost somberly, in an austere gray jumpsuit.

"I feel it," he said, clutching d'Branin by the arm, his long fingernails digging in painfully. "Something is wrong, Karoly, something is very wrong. I'm beginning to get frightened."

The telepath's nails bit, and d'Branin pulled away hard. "You are hurting me," he protested. "My friend, what is it? Frightened? Of what, of whom? I do not understand. What could there be to fear?"

Lasamer raised pale hands to his face. "I don't know, I don't *know*," he wailed. "Yet it's *there*, I feel it. Karoly, I'm picking up something. You know I'm good, I am, that's why you picked me. Just a moment ago, when my nails dug into you, I felt it. I can read you now, in flashes. You're thinking I'm too excitable, that it's the confinement, that I've got to be calmed down." The young man laughed a thin hysterical laugh that died as quickly as it had begun. "No, you see, I am good. Class one, tested, and I tell you I'm afraid. I sense it. Feel it. Dream of it. I felt it even as we were boarding, and it's gotten worse. Something dangerous. Something volatile. And alien, Karoly, *alien*!"

"The *volcryn*!" d'Branin said.

"No, impossible. We're in drive, they're light-years away." The edgy laughter sounded again. "I'm not that good, Karoly. I've heard your Crey story, but I'm only a human. No, this is close. On the ship."

"One of us?"

"Maybe," Lasamer said. He rubbed his cheek absently. "I can't sort it out."

D'Branin put a fatherly hand on his shoulder. "Thale, this feeling of yours—could it be that you are just tired? We have all of us been under strain. Inactivity can be taxing."

"Get your hand off me," Lasamer snapped.

D'Branin drew back his hand quickly.

"This is *real,*" the telepath insisted, "and I don't need you thinking that maybe you shouldn't have taken me, all that crap. I'm as stable as anyone on this . . . this . . . how *dare* you think I'm unstable, you ought to look inside some of these others, Christopheris with his bottle and his dirty little fantasies, Dannel half sick with fear, Lommie and her machines, with her it's all metal and lights and cool circuits, sick, I tell you, and Jhirl's arrogant and Agatha whines even in her head to herself all the time, and Alys is empty, like a cow. You, you don't touch them, see into them, what do you know of *stable*? Losers, d'Branin, they've given you a bunch of losers, and I'm one of your best, so don't you go thinking that I'm not stable, not sane, you hear." His blue eyes were fevered. "Do you *hear*?"

"Easy," d'Branin said. "Easy, Thale, you're getting excited."

The telepath blinked, and suddenly the wildness was gone. "Excited?" he said. "Yes." He looked around guiltily. "It's hard, Karoly, but listen to me, you must, I'm warning you. We're in danger."

"I will listen," d'Branin said, "but I cannot act without more definite information. You must use your talent and get it for me, yes? You can do that."

Lasamer nodded. "Yes," he said. "Yes." They talked quietly for more than an hour, and finally the telepath left peacefully.

Afterwards d'Branin went straight to the psipsych, who was lying in her sleepweb surrounded by medicines, complaining bitterly of aches. "Interesting," she said when d'Branin told her. "I've felt something, too, a sense of threat, very vague, diffuse. I thought it was me, the confinement, the boredom, the way I feel. My moods betray me at times. Did he say anything more specific?"

"No."

"I'll make an effort to move around, read him, read the others, see what I can pick up. Although, if this is real, he should know it first. He's a one, I'm only a three."

D'Branin nodded. "He seems very receptive," he said. "He told me all kinds of things about the others."

"Means nothing. Sometimes, when a telepath insists he is picking up everything, what it means is that he's picking up nothing at all. He imagines feelings, readings, to make up for those that will not come. I'll keep careful watch on him, d'Branin. Sometimes a talent can crack, slip into a kind of hysteria, and begin to broadcast instead of receive. In a closed environment, that's very dangerous."

Karoly d'Branin nodded. "Of course, of course."

In another part of the ship, Royd Eris frowned.

"Have you noticed the clothing on that holograph he sends us?" Rojan Christopheris asked Alys Northwind. They were alone in one of the holds, reclining on a mat, trying to avoid the wet spot. The xenobiologist had lit a joystick. He offered it to his companion, but Northwind waved it away.

"A decade out of style, maybe more. My father wore shirts like that when he was a boy on Old Poseidon."

"Eris has old-fashioned taste," Alys Northwind said.

"So? I don't care what he wears. Me, I like my jumpsuits. They're comfortable. Don't care what people think."

"You don't, do you?" Christopheris said, wrinkling his huge nose. She did not see the gesture. "Well, you miss the point. What if that isn't really Eris? A projection can be anything, can be made up out of whole cloth. I don't think he really looks like that."

"No?" Now her voice was curious. She rolled over and curled up beneath his arm, her heavy white breasts against his chest.

"What if he's sick, deformed, ashamed to be seen the way he really looks?" Christopheris said. "Perhaps he has some disease. The Slow Plague can waste a person terribly, but it takes decades to kill, and there are other contagions—manthrax, new leprosy, the melt, Langamen's Disease, lots of them. Could be that Royd's self-imposed quarantine is just that. A quarantine. Think about it."

Alys Northwind frowned. "All this talk of Eris," she said, "is making me edgy."

The xenobiologist sucked on his joystick and laughed. "Welcome to the *Nightflyer,* then. The rest of us are already there."

* * *

In the fifth week out, Melantha Jhirl pushed her pawn to the sixth rank and Royd saw that it was unstoppable and resigned. It was his eighth straight defeat at her hands in as many days. She was sitting cross-legged on the floor of the lounge, the chessmen spread out before her in front of a darkened viewscreen. Laughing, she swept them all away. "Don't feel bad, Royd," she told him. "I'm an improved model. Always three moves ahead."

"I should tie in my computer," he replied. "You'd never know." His ghost materialized suddenly, standing in front of the viewscreen, and smiled at her.

"I'd know within three moves," Melantha Jhirl said. "Try it."

They were the last victims of a chess fever that had swept the *Nightflyer* for more than a week. Initially it had been Christopheris who produced the set and urged people to play, but the others had lost interest quickly when Thale Lasamer sat down and beat them all, one by one. Everyone was certain that he'd done it by reading their minds, but the telepath was in a volatile, nasty mood, and no one dared voice the accusation. Melantha, however, had been able to defeat Lasamer without very much trouble. "He isn't that good a player," she told Royd afterwards, "and if he's trying to lift ideas from me, he's getting gibberish. The improved model knows certain mental disciplines. I can shield myself well enough, thank you." Christopheris and a few of the others then tried a game or two against Melantha, and were routed for their troubles. Finally Royd asked if he might play. Only Melantha and Karoly were willing to sit down with him over the board, and since Karoly could barely recall how the pieces moved from one moment to the next, that left Melantha and Royd as regular opponents. They both seemed to thrive on the games, though Melantha always won.

Melantha stood up and walked to the kitchen, stepping right through Royd's ghostly form, which she steadfastly refused to pretend was real. "The rest of them walk around me," Royd complained.

She shrugged, and found a bulb of beer in a storage compartment. "When are you going to break down and let me behind your wall for a visit, captain?" she asked. "Don't you get lonely back there? Sexually frustrated? Claustrophobic?"

"I have flown the *Nightflyer* all my life, Melantha," Royd said. His projection, ignored, winked out. "If I were subject to claustrophobia, sexual frustration, or loneliness, such a life would have been impossible.

Surely that should be obvious to you, being as improved a model as you are?"

She took a squeeze of her beer and laughed her mellow, musical laugh at him. "I'll solve you yet, captain," she warned.

"Meanwhile," he said, "tell me some more lies about your life."

"Have you ever heard of Jupiter?" the xenotech demanded of the others. She was drunk, lolling in her sleepweb in the cargo hold.

"Something to do with Earth," said Lindran. "The same myth system originated both names, I believe."

"Jupiter," the xenotech announced loudly, "is a gas giant in the same solar system as Old Earth. Didn't know that, did you?"

"I've got more important things to occupy my mind than such trivia, Alys," Lindran said.

Alys Northwind smiled down smugly. "Listen, I'm talking to you. They were on the verge of exploring this Jupiter when the stardrive was discovered, oh, way back. After that, course, no one bothered with gas giants. Just slip into drive and find the habitable worlds, settle them, ignore the comets and the rocks and the gas giants—there's another star just a few light-years away, and it has *more* habitable planets. But there were people who thought those Jupiters might have life, you know. Do you see?"

"I see that you're blind drunk," Lindran said.

Christopheris looked annoyed. "If there is intelligent life on the gas giants, it shows no interest in leaving them," he snapped. "All of the sentient species we have met up to now have originated on worlds similar to Earth, and most of them are oxygen breathers. Unless you're suggesting that the *volcryn* are from a gas giant?"

The xenotech pushed herself up to a sitting position and smiled conspiratorially. "Not the *volcryn*," she said. "Royd Eris. Crack that forward bulkhead in the lounge, and watch the methane and ammonia come smoking out." Her hand made a sensuous waving motion through the air, and she convulsed with giddy laughter.

The system was up and running. Cyberneticist Lommie Thorne sat at the master console, a featureless black plastic plate upon which the phantom images of a hundred keyboard configurations came and went in holographic display, vanishing and shifting even as she used them. Around her rose crystalline data grids, ranks of viewscreens and readout panels upon which columns of figures marched and geometric shapes did stately whirling dances, dark columns of seamless metal that contained the mind and soul of her system. She sat in the semi-darkness happily, whistling as she ran the computer through several simple routines, her fingers moving across the flickering keys with blind speed and quickening tempo. "Ah," she said once, smiling. Later, only, "Good."

Then it was time for the final run-through. Lommie Thorne slid back the metallic fabric of her left sleeve, pushed her wrist beneath the console, found the prongs, jacked herself in. Interface.

Ecstasy.

Inkblot shapes in a dozen glowing colors twisted and melded and broke apart on the readout screens.

In an instant it was over.

Lommie Thorne pulled free her wrist. The smile on her face was shy and satisfied, but across it lay another expression, the merest hint of puzzlement. She touched her thumb to the holes of her wrist jack, and found them warm to the touch, tingling. Lommie shivered.

The system was running perfectly, hardware in good condition, all software systems functioning according to plan, interface meshing well. It had been a delight, as it always was. When she joined with the system, she was wise beyond her years, and powerful, and full of light and electricity and the stuff of life, cool and clean and exciting to touch, and never alone, never small or weak. That was what it was always like when she interfaced and let herself expand.

But this time something had been different. Something cold had touched her, only for a moment. Something very cold and very frightening, and together she and the system had seen it clearly for a brief moment, and then it had been gone again.

The cyberneticist shook her head, and drove the nonsense out. She went back to work. After a time, she began to whistle.

During the sixth week, Alys Northwind cut herself badly while preparing a snack. She was standing in the kitchen, slicing a spiced meatstick with a long knife, when suddenly she screamed.

Dannel and Lindran rushed to her, and found her staring down in horror at the chopping block in front of her. The knife had taken off the first joint of the index finger on her left hand, and the blood was spreading in ragged spurts. "The ship lurched," Alys said numbly, staring up at Dannel. "Didn't you feel it jerk? It pushed the knife to the side."

"Get something to stop the bleeding," Lindran said. Dannel looked around in panic. "Oh, I'll do it myself," Lindran finally said, and she did.

The psipsych, Agatha Marij-Black, gave Northwind a tranquilizer, then looked at the two linguists. "Did you see it happen?"

"She did it herself, with the knife," Dannel said.

From somewhere down the corridor, there came the sound of wild, hysterical laughter.

"I dampened him," Marij-Black reported to Karoly d'Branin later the same day. "Psionine-4. It will blunt his receptivity for several days, and I have more if he needs it."

D'Branin wore a stricken look. "We talked several times and I could see that Thale was becoming ever more fearful, but he could never tell me the why of it. Did you have to shut him off?"

The psipsych shrugged. "He was edging into the irrational. Given his level of talent, if he'd gone over the edge he might have taken us all with him. You should never have taken a class one telepath, d'Branin. Too unstable."

"We must communicate with an alien race. I remind you that is no easy task. The *volcryn* will be more alien than any sentients we have yet encountered. We needed class one skills if we were to have any hope of reaching them. And they have so much to teach us, my friend!"

"Glib," she said, "but you might have no working skills at all, given the condition of your class one. Half the time he's curled up into the fetal position in his sleepweb, half the time he's strutting and crowing and half mad with fear. He insists we're all in real physical danger, but he doesn't know why or from what. The worst of it is that I can't tell if he's really sensing something or simply having an acute attack of paranoia. He certainly displays some classic paranoid symptoms. Among other things, he insists that he's being watched. Perhaps his condition is completely unrelated to us, the *volcryn,* and his talent. I can't be sure."

"What of your own talent?" d'Branin said. "You are an empath, are you not?"

"Don't tell me my job," she said sharply. "I sexed with him last week. You don't get more proximity or better rapport for esping than that. Even under those conditions, I couldn't be sure of anything. His mind is a chaos, and his fear is so rank it stank up the sheets. I don't read anything from the others either, besides the ordinary tensions and frustrations. But I'm only a three, so that doesn't mean much. My abilities are limited. You know I haven't been feeling well, d'Branin. I can barely breathe on this ship. The air seems thick and heavy to me, my head throbs. I ought to stay in bed."

"Yes, of course," d'Branin said hastily. "I did not mean to criticize. You have been doing all you can under difficult circumstances. How long will it be until Thale is with us again?"

The psipsych rubbed her temple wearily. "I'm recommending we keep him dampened until the mission is over, d'Branin. I warn you, an insane or hysterical telepath is dangerous. That business with Northwind and the knife might have been his doing, you know. He started screaming not long after, remember. Maybe he'd touched her, for just an instant—oh, it's a wild idea, but it's possible. The point is, we don't take chances. I have enough psionine-4 to keep him numb and functional until we're back on Avalon."

"*But*—Royd will take us out of drive soon, and we will make contact with the *volcryn*. We will need Thale, his mind, his talent. Is it vital to keep him dampened? Is there no other way?"

Marij-Black grimaced. "My other option was an injection of esperon. It would have opened him up completely, increased his psionic receptivity tenfold for a few hours. Then, I'd hope, he could focus in on this danger he's feeling. Exorcise it if it's false, deal with it if it's real. But psionine-4 is a lot safer. Esperon is a hell of a drug, with devastating side effects. It raises the blood pressure dramatically, sometimes brings on hyperventilation or seizures, has even been known to stop the heart. Lasamer is young enough so that I'm not worried about that, but I don't think he has the emotional stability to deal with that kind of power. The psionine should tell us something. If his paranoia persists, I'll know it has nothing to do with his telepathy."

"And if it does not persist?" Karoly d'Branin said.

Agatha Marij-Black smiled wickedly at him. "If Lasamer becomes quiescent, and stops babbling about danger? Why, that would mean he was no longer picking up anything, wouldn't it? And *that* would mean there had been something to pick up, that he'd been right all along."

At dinner that night, Thale Lasamer was quiet and distracted, eating in a rhythmic, mechanical sort of way, with a cloudy look in his blue eyes. Afterwards he excused himself and went straight to bed, falling into exhausted slumber almost immediately.

"What did you do to him?" Lommie Thorne asked Marij-Black.

"I shut off that prying mind of his," she replied.

"You should have done it two weeks ago," Lindran said. "Docile, he's a lot easier to take."

Karoly d'Branin hardly touched his food.

False night came, and Royd's wraith materialized while Karoly d'Branin sat brooding over his chocolate. "Karoly," the apparition said, "would it be possible to tie in the computer your team brought on board with my shipboard system? Your *volcryn* stories fascinate me, and I would like to be able to study them further at my leisure. I assume the details of your investigation are in storage."

"Certainly," d'Branin replied in an offhand, distracted manner. "Our system is up now. Patching it into the *Nightflyer* should present no problem. I will tell Lommie to attend to it tomorrow."

Silence hung in the room heavily. Karoly d'Branin sipped at his chocolate and stared off into the darkness, almost unaware of Royd.

"You are troubled," Royd said after a time.

"Eh? Oh, yes." D'Branin looked up. "Forgive me, my friend. I have much on my mind."

"It concerns Thale Lasamer, does it not?"

Karoly d'Branin looked at the pale, luminescent figure across from him for a long time before he finally managed a stiff nod. "Yes. Might I ask how you knew that?"

"I know everything that occurs on the *Nightflyer*," Royd said.

"You have been watching us," d'Branin said gravely, accusation in his tone. "Then it is so, what Thale says, about us being watched. Royd, how could you? Spying is beneath you."

The ghost's transparent eyes had no life in them, did not see. "Do not tell the others," Royd warned. "Karoly, my friend—if I may call you my friend—I have my own reasons for watching, reasons it would not profit you to know. I mean you no harm. Believe that. You have hired me to take you safely to the *volcryn* and safely back, and I mean to do just that."

"You are being evasive, Royd," d'Branin said. "Why do you spy on us? Do you watch everything? Are you a voyeur, some enemy, is that why you do not mix with us? Is watching all you intend to do?"

"Your suspicions hurt me, Karoly."

"Your deception hurts me. Will you not answer me?"

"I have eyes and ears everywhere," Royd said. "There

is no place to hide from me on the *Nightflyer*. Do I see everything? No, not always. I am only human, no matter what your colleagues might think. I sleep. The monitors remain on, but there is no one to observe them. I can only pay attention to one or two scenes or inputs at once. Sometimes I grow distracted, unobservant. I watch everything, Karoly, but I do not see everything."

"Why?" D'Branin poured himself a fresh cup of chocolate, steadying his hand with an effort.

"I do not have to answer that question. The *Nightflyer* is my ship."

D'Branin sipped chocolate, blinked, nodded to himself. "You grieve me, my friend. You give me no choice. Thale said we were being watched. I now learn that he was right. He says also that we are in danger. Something alien, he says. You?"

The projection was still and silent.

D'Branin clucked. "You do not answer. Ah, Royd, what am I to do? I must believe him, then. We are in danger, perhaps from you. I must abort our mission, then. Return us to Avalon, Royd. That is my decision."

The ghost smiled wanly. "So close, Karoly? Soon now we will be dropping out of drive."

Karoly d'Branin made a small, sad noise deep in his throat. "My *volcryn*," he said, sighing. "So close—ah, it pains me to desert them. But I cannot do otherwise, I cannot."

"You can," said the voice of Royd Eris. "Trust me. That is all I ask, Karoly. Believe me when I tell you that I have no sinister intentions. Thale Lasamer may speak of danger, but no one has been harmed so far, have they?"

"No," admitted d'Branin. "No, unless you count Alys, cutting herself this afternoon."

"What?" Royd hesitated briefly. "Cutting herself? I did not see, Karoly. When did this happen?"

"Oh, early—just before Lasamer began to scream and rant, I believe."

"I see." Royd's voice was thoughtful. "I was watching Melantha go through her exercises," he said finally, "and talking to her. I did not notice. Tell me how it happened."

D'Branin told him.

"Listen to me," Royd said. "Trust me, Karoly, and I will give you your *volcryn*. Calm your people. Assure them that I am no threat. And keep Lasamer drugged and quiescent, do you understand? That is very important. He is the problem."

"Agatha advises much the same thing."

"I know," said Royd. "I agree with her. Will you do as I ask?"

"I do not know," d'Branin said. "You make it hard for me. I do not understand what is going wrong, my friend. Will you not tell me more?"

Royd Eris did not answer. His ghost waited.

"Well," d'Branin said at last, "you do not talk. How difficult you make it. How soon, Royd? How soon will we see my *volcryn*?"

"Quite soon," Royd replied. "We will drop out of drive in approximately seventy hours."

"Seventy hours," d'Branin said. "Such a short time. Going back would gain us nothing." He moistened his lips, lifted his cup, found it empty. "Go on, then. I will do as you bid. I will trust you, keep Lasamer drugged, I will not tell the others of your spying. Is that enough, then? Give me my *volcryn*. I have waited so long!"

"I know," said Royd Eris. "I know."

Then the ghost was gone, and Karoly d'Branin sat alone in the darkened lounge. He tried to refill his cup, but his hand began to tremble unaccountably, and he poured the chocolate over his fingers and dropped the cup, swearing, wondering, hurting.

* * *

The next day was a day of rising tensions and a hundred small irritations. Lindran and Dannel had a "private" argument that could be overheard through half the ship. A three-handed war game in the lounge ended in disaster when Christopheris accused Melantha Jhirl of cheating. Lommie Thorne complained of unusual difficulties in tying her system into the shipboard computers. Alys Northwind sat in the lounge for hours, staring at her bandaged finger with a look of sullen hatred on her face. Agatha Marij-Black prowled through the corridors, complaining that the ship was too hot, that her joints throbbed, that the air was thick and full of smoke, that the ship was too cold. Even Karoly d'Branin was despondent and on edge.

Only the telepath seemed content. Shot full of psionine-4, Thale Lasamer was often sluggish and lethargic, but at least he no longer flinched at shadows.

Royd Eris made no appearance, either by voice or holographic projection.

He was still absent at dinner. The academicians ate uneasily, expecting him to materialize at any moment, take his accustomed place, and join in the mealtime conversation. Their expectations were still unfulfilled when the after-dinner pots of chocolate and spiced tea and coffee were set on the table.

"Our captain seems to be occupied," Melantha Jhirl observed, leaning back in her chair and swirling a snifter of brandy.

"We will be shifting out of drive soon," Karoly d'Branin said. "Undoubtedly there are preparations to make." Secretly, he fretted over Royd's absence, and wondered if they were being watched even now.

Rojan Christopheris cleared his throat. "Since we're all here and he's not, perhaps this is a good time to discuss certain things. I'm not concerned about him missing dinner. He doesn't eat. He's a damned hologram. What does it matter? Maybe it's just as well, we need to talk about this. Karoly, a lot of us have been getting uneasy about Royd Eris. What do you know about this mystery man, anyway?"

"Know, my friend?" D'Branin refilled his cup with the thick bittersweet chocolate and sipped at it slowly, trying to give himself a moment to think. "What is there to know?"

"Surely you've noticed that he never comes out to play with us," Lindran said drily. "Before you engaged his ship, did anyone remark on this quirk of his?"

"I'd like to know the answer to that one, too," said Dannel, the other linguist. "A lot of traffic comes and goes through Avalon. How did you come to choose Eris? What were you told about him?"

"Told about him? Very little, I must admit. I spoke to a few port officials and charter companies, but none of them were acquainted with Royd. He had not traded out of Avalon originally, you see."

"How convenient," said Lindran.

"How suspicious," added Dannel.

"Where *is* he from, then?" Lindran demanded. "Dannel and I have listened to him pretty carefully. He speaks standard very flatly, with no discernible accent, no idiosyncrasies to betray his origins."

"Sometimes he sounds a bit archaic," Dannel put in, "and from time to time one of his constructions will give me an association. Only it's a different one each time. He's traveled a lot."

"Such a deduction," Lindran said, patting his hand. "Traders frequently do, love. Comes of owning a starship."

Dannel glared at her, but Lindran just went on. "Seriously, though, do you know anything about him? Where did this *Nightflyer* of ours come from?"

"I do not know," d'Branin admitted. "I—I never thought to ask." The members of his research team glanced at one another incredulously.

"You never thought to *ask*?" Christopheris said. "How did you come to select this ship?"

"It was available. The administrative council approved my project and assigned me personnel, but they could not spare an Academy ship. There were budgetary constraints as well."

Agatha Marij-Black laughed sourly. "What d'Branin is telling those of you who haven't figured it out is that the Academy was pleased with his studies in xenomyth, with the discovery of the *volcryn* legend, but less than enthusiastic about his plan to seek them out. So they gave him a small budget to keep him happy and productive, assuming this little mission would be fruitless, and they assigned him people who wouldn't be missed back on Avalon." She looked around. "Look at the lot of you. None of us had worked with d'Branin in the early stages, but we were all available for this jaunt. And not a one of us is a first-rate scholar."

"Speak for yourself," Melantha Jhirl said. "I volunteered for this mission."

"I won't argue the point," the psipsych said. "The

crux is that the choice of the *Nightflyer* is no large enigma. You just engaged the cheapest charter you could find, didn't you, d'Branin?"

"Some of the available ships would not consider my proposition," d'Branin said. "The sound of it is odd, we must admit. And many shipmasters have an almost superstitious fear of dropping out of drive in interstellar space, without a planet near. Of those who would agree to the conditions, Royd Eris offered the best terms, and he was able to leave at once."

"And we *had* to leave at once," said Lindran. "Otherwise the *volcryn* might get away. They've only been passing through this region for ten thousand years, give or take a few thousand."

Someone laughed. D'Branin was nonplussed. "Friends, no doubt I could have postponed departure. I admit I was eager to meet my *volcryn,* to see their great ships and ask them all the questions that have haunted me, to discover the why of them. But I admit also that a delay would have been no great hardship. But why? Royd has been a gracious host, a good pilot. We have been treated well."

"Did you meet him?" Alys Northwind asked. "When you were making your arrangements, did you ever see him?"

"We spoke many times, but I was on Avalon, and Royd in orbit. I saw his face on my viewscreen."

"A projection, a computer simulation, could be anything," Lommie Thorne said. "I can have my system conjure up all sorts of faces for your viewscreen, Karoly."

"No one has ever seen this Royd Eris," Christopheris said. "He has made himself a cipher from the start."

"Our host wishes his privacy to remain inviolate," d'Branin said.

"Evasions," Lindran said. "What is he hiding?"

Melantha Jhirl laughed. When all eyes had moved to her, she grinned and shook her head. "Captain Royd is perfect, a strange man for a strange mission. Don't any of you love a mystery? Here we are flying light-years to intercept a hypothetical alien starship from the core of the galaxy that has been outward-bound for longer than humanity has been having wars, and all of you are upset because you can't count the warts on Royd's nose." She leaned across the table to refill her brandy snifter. "My mother was right," she said lightly. "Normals are subnormal."

"Maybe we should listen to Melantha," Lommie Thorne said thoughtfully. "Royd's foibles and neuroses are his business, if he does not impose them on us."

"It makes me uncomfortable," Dannel complained weakly.

"For all we know," said Alys Northwind, "we might be traveling with a criminal or an alien."

"Jupiter," someone muttered. The xenotech flushed red and there was sniggering around the long table.

But Thale Lasamer looked up furtively from his plate, and giggled. "An *alien,*" he said. His blue eyes flicked back and forth in his skull, as if seeking escape. They were bright and wild.

Marij-Black swore. "The drug is wearing off," she said quickly to d'Branin. "I'll have to go back to my cabin to get some more."

"What drug?" Lommie Thorne demanded. D'Branin had been careful not to tell the others too much about Lasamer's ravings, for fear of inflaming the shipboard tensions. "What's going on?"

"Danger," Lasamer said. He turned to Lommie, sitting next to him, and grasped her forearm hard, his long, painted fingernails clawing at the silvery metal of her shirt. "We're in danger, I tell you, I'm reading it. Something *alien.* It means us ill. Blood, I see blood." He laughed. "Can you taste it, Agatha? I can almost taste the blood. *It* can, too."

Marij-Black rose. "He's not well," she announced to

the others. "I've been dampening him with psionine, trying to hold his delusions in check. I'll get some more." She started towards the door.

"Dampening him?" Christopheris said, horrified. "He's warning us of something. Don't you hear him? I want to know what it *is*."

"Not psionine," said Melantha Jhirl. "Try esperon."

"Don't tell me my job, woman!"

"Sorry," Melantha said. She gave a modest shrug. "I'm one step ahead of you, though. Esperon might exorcise his delusions, no?"

"Yes, but—"

"And it might help him focus on this threat he claims to detect, correct?"

"I know the characteristics of esperon quite well," the psipsych said testily.

Melantha smiled over the rim of her brandy glass. "I'm sure you do. Now listen to me. All of you are anxious about Royd, it seems. You can't stand not knowing whatever it is he's concealing. Rojan has been making up stories for weeks, and he's ready to believe any of them. Alys is so nervous she cut her finger off. We're squabbling constantly. Fears like that won't help us work together as a team. Let's end them. Easy enough." She pointed to Thale. "Here sits a class one telepath.

Boost his power with esperon and he'll be able to recite our captain's life history to us, until we're all suitably bored with it. Meanwhile he'll also be vanquishing his personal demons."

"He's watching us," the telepath said in a low, urgent voice.

"No," said Karoly d'Branin, "we must keep Thale dampened."

"Karoly," Christopheris said, "this has gone too far. Several of us are nervous and this boy is terrified. I believe we all need an end to the mystery of Royd Eris. For once, Melantha is right."

"We have no right," d'Branin said.

"We have the need," said Lommie Thorne. "I agree with Melantha."

"Yes," echoed Alys Northwind. The two linguists were nodding.

D'Branin thought regretfully of his promise to Royd. They were not giving him any choice. His eyes met those of the psipsych, and he sighed. "Do it, then," he said. "Get him the esperon."

"He's going to kill me." Thale Lasamer screamed. He leapt to his feet, and when Lommie Thorne tried to calm him with a hand on his arm, he seized a cup of coffee

and threw it square in her face. It took three of them to hold him down.

"Hurry," Christopheris barked, as the telepath struggled.

Marij-Black shuddered and left the lounge.

When she returned, the others had lifted Lasamer to the table and forced him down, pulling aside his long pale hair to bare the arteries in his neck.

Marij-Black moved to his side.

"Stop that," Royd said. "There is no need."

His ghost shimmered into being in its empty chair at the head of the long dinner table. The psipsych froze in the act of slipping an ampule of esperon into her injection gun, and Alys Northwind startled visibly and released one of Lasamer's arms. The captive did not pull free. He lay on the table, breathing heavily, his pale blue eyes fixed glassily on Royd's projection, transfixed by the vision of his sudden materialization.

Melantha Jhirl lifted her brandy glass in salute. "Boo," she said. "You've missed dinner, captain."

"Royd," said Karoly d'Branin, "I am sorry."

The ghost stared unseeing at the far wall. "Release

him," said the voice from the communicators. "I will tell you my great secrets, if my privacy intimidates you so."

"He *has* been watching us," Dannel said.

"We're listening," Northwind said suspiciously. "What are you?"

"I liked your guess about the gas giants," Royd said. "Sadly, the truth is less dramatic. I am an ordinary *Homo sapien* in middle age. Sixty-eight standard, if you require precision. The hologram you see before you is the real Royd Eris, or was so some years ago. I am somewhat older now, but I use computer simulation to project a more youthful appearance to my guests."

"Oh?" Lommie Thorne's face was red where the coffee had scalded her. "Then why the secrecy?"

"I will begin the tale with my mother," Royd replied. "The *Nightflyer* was her ship originally, custom-built to her design in the Newholme spaceyards. My mother was a freetrader, a notably successful one. She was born trash on a world called Vess, which is a very long way from here, although perhaps some of you have heard of it. She worked her way up, position by position, until she won her own command. She soon made a fortune through a willingness to accept the unusual consignment, fly off the major trade routes, take her cargo a month or a year or two years beyond where it was

customarily transferred. Such practices are riskier but more profitable than flying the mail runs. My mother did not worry about how often she and her crews returned home. Her ships were her home. She forgot about Vess as soon as she left it, and seldom visited the same world twice if she could avoid it."

"Adventurous," Melantha Jhirl said.

"No," said Royd. "Sociopathic. My mother did not like people, you see. Not at all. Her crews had no love for her, nor she for them. Her one great dream was to free herself from the necessity of crew altogether. When she grew rich enough, she had it done. The *Nightflyer* was the result. After she boarded it at Newholme, she never touched a human being again, or walked a planet's surface. She did all her business from the compartments that are now mine, by viewscreen or lasercom. You would call her insane. You would be right." The ghost smiled faintly. "She did have an interesting life, though, even after her isolation. The worlds she saw, Karoly! The things she might have told you would break your heart, but you'll never hear them. She destroyed most of her records for fear that other people might get some use or pleasure from her experiences after her death. She was like that."

"And you?" asked Alys Northwind.

"She must have touched at least *one* other human being," Lindran put in, with a smile.

"I should not call her my mother," Royd said. "I am her cross-sex clone. After thirty years of flying this ship alone, she was bored. I was to be her companion and lover. She could shape me to be a perfect diversion. She had no patience with children, however, and no desire to raise me herself. After she had done the cloning, I was sealed in a nurturant tank, an embryo linked into her computer. It was my teacher. Before birth and after. I had no birth, really. Long after the time a normal child would have been born, I remained in the tank, growing, learning, on slow-time, blind and dreaming and living through tubes. I was to be released when I had attained the age of puberty, at which time she guessed I would be fit company."

"How horrible," Karoly d'Branin said. "Royd, my friend, I did not know."

"I'm sorry, captain," Melantha Jhirl said. "You were robbed of your childhood."

"I never missed it," Royd said. "Nor her. Her plans were all futile, you see. She died a few months after the cloning, when I was still a fetus in the tank. She had programmed the ship for such an eventuality, however. It dropped out of drive and shut down, drifted in interstellar space for eleven standard years while the computer made me—" He stopped, smiling. "I was going to say *while the computer made me a human being.* Well, while the computer made me whatever I am, then. That was how I inherited the *Nightflyer.* When I was born, it took me some months to acquaint myself with the operation of the ship and my own origins."

"Fascinating," said Karoly d'Branin.

"Yes," said the linguist Lindran, "but it doesn't explain why you keep yourself in isolation."

"Ah, but it does," Melantha Jhirl said. "Captain, perhaps you should explain further for the less-improved models?"

"My mother hated planets," Royd said. "She hated stinks and dirt and bacteria, the irregularity of the weather, the sight of other people. She engineered for us a flawless environment, as sterile as she could possibly make it. She disliked gravity as well. She was accustomed to weightlessness from years of service on ancient freetraders that could not afford gravity grids, and she preferred it. These were the conditions under which I was born and raised.

"My body has no immune systems, no natural resistance to anything. Contact with any of you would probably kill me, and would certainly make me very sick.

My muscles are feeble, in a sense atrophied. The gravity the *Nightflyer* is now generating is for your comfort, not mine. To me it is agony. At this moment the real me is seated in a floating chair that supports my weight. I still hurt, and my internal organs may be suffering damage. It is one reason why I do not often take on passengers."

"You share your mother's opinion of the run of humanity?" asked Marij-Black.

"I do not. I like people. I accept what I am, but I did not choose it. I experience human life in the only way I can, vicariously. I am a voracious consumer of books, tapes, holoplays, fictions and drama and histories of all sorts. I have experimented with dreamdust. And infrequently, when I dare, I carry passengers. At those times, I drink in as much of their lives as I can."

"If you kept your ship under weightlessness at all times, you could take on more riders," suggested Lommie Thorne.

"True," Royd said politely. "I have found, however, that most planet-born are as uncomfortable weightless as I am under gravity. A shipmaster who does not have artificial gravity, or elects not to use it, attracts few riders. The exceptions often spend much of the voyage sick or drugged. No. I could also mingle with my passengers, I know, if I kept to my chair and wore a sealed environ-wear suit. I have done so. I find it lessens my participation instead of increasing it. I become a freak, a maimed thing, one who must be treated differently and kept at a distance. These things do not suit my purpose. I prefer isolation. As often as I dare, I study the aliens I take on as riders."

"Aliens?" Northwind's voice was confused.

"You are all aliens to me," Royd answered.

Silence filled the *Nightflyer's* lounge.

"I am sorry this has happened, my friend," Karoly d'Branin said. "We ought not have intruded on your personal affairs."

"Sorry," muttered Agatha Marij-Black. She frowned and pushed the ampule of esperon into the injection chamber. "Well, it's glib enough, but is it the truth? We still have no proof, just a new bedtime story. The hologram could have claimed it was a creature from Jupiter, a computer, or a diseased war criminal just as easily. We have no way of verifying anything that he's said. No— we have one way, rather." She took two quick steps forward to where Thale Lasamer lay on the table. "He still needs treatment and we still need confirmation, and I don't see any sense in stopping now after we've gone this far. Why should we live with all this anxiety if we can end it all now?" Her hand pushed the telepath's unresisting head to one side. She found the artery and pressed the gun to it.

"Agatha," said Karoly d'Branin. "Don't you think . . . perhaps we should forgo this, now that Royd . . . ?"

"NO," Royd said. "Stop. I order it. This is my ship. Stop, or . . ."

". . . or what?" The gun hissed loudly, and there was a red mark on the telepath's neck when she lifted it away.

Lasamer raised himself to a half-sitting position, supported by his elbows, and Marij-Black moved close to him. "Thale," she said in her best professional tone, "focus on Royd. You can do it, we all know how good you are. Wait just a moment, the esperon will open it all up for you."

His pale blue eyes were clouded. "Not close enough," he muttered. "One, I'm one, tested. Good, you know I'm good, but I got to be *close*." He trembled.

The psipsych put an arm around him, stroked him, coaxed him. "The esperon will give you range, Thale," she said. "Feel it, feel yourself grow stronger. Can you feel it? Everything's getting clear, isn't it?" Her voice was a reassuring drone. "You can hear what I'm thinking, I know you can, but never mind that. The others, too, push them aside, all that chatter, thoughts, desires, fear. Push it all aside. Remember the danger now? Remember? Go find it, Thale, go find the danger. Look beyond the wall there, tell us what it's like beyond the wall. Tell us about Royd. Was he telling the truth? Tell us. You're good, we all know that, you can tell us." The phrases were almost an incantation.

He shrugged off her support and sat upright by himself. "I can feel it," he said. His eyes were suddenly clearer. "Something—my head hurts—I'm *afraid*!"

"Don't be afraid," said Marij-Black. "The esperon won't make your head hurt, it just makes you better. We're all here with you. Nothing to fear." She stroked his brow. "Tell us what you see."

Thale Lasamer looked at Royd's ghost with terrified little-boy eyes, and his tongue flicked across his lower lips. "He's—"

Then his skull exploded.

Hysteria and confusion.

The telepath's head had burst with awful force, splattering them all with blood and bits of bone and flesh. His body thrashed madly on the tabletop for a long instant, blood spurting from the arteries in his neck in a crimson stream, his limbs twitching in a macabre dance.

His head had simply ceased to exist, but he would not be still.

Agatha Marij-Black, who had been standing closest to him, dropped her injection gun and stood slack-mouthed. She was drenched with his blood, covered with pieces of flesh and brain. Beneath her right eye, a long sliver of bone had penetrated her skin, and her own blood was mingling with his. She did not seem to notice.

Rojan Christopheris fell over backward, scrambled to his feet, and pressed himself hard against the wall.

Dannel screamed, and screamed, and screamed, until Lindran slapped him hard across a blood-smeared cheek and told him to be quiet.

Alys Northwind dropped to her knees and began to mumble a prayer in a strange tongue.

Karoly d'Branin sat very still, staring, blinking, his chocolate cup forgotten in his hand.

"Do something," Lommie Thorne moaned. "Somebody *do* something." One of Lasamer's arms moved feebly, and brushed against her. She shrieked and pulled away.

Melantha Jhirl pushed aside her brandy snifter. "Control yourself," she snapped. "He's dead, he can't hurt you."

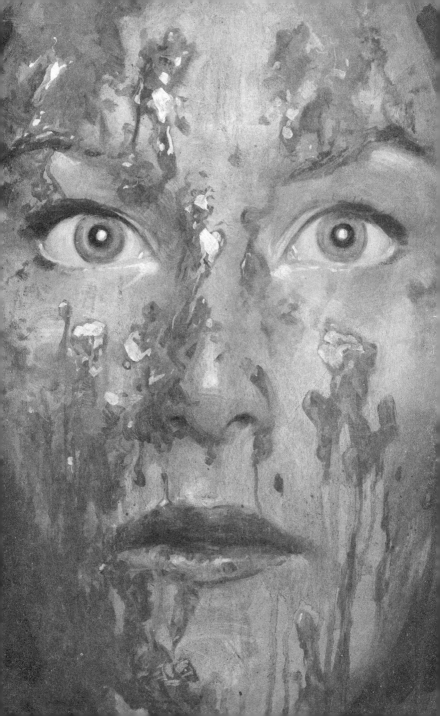

They all looked at her but for d'Branin and Marij-Black, both of whom seemed frozen in shock. Royd's projection had vanished at some point, Melantha realized suddenly. She began to give orders. "Dannel, Lindran, Rojan—find a sheet or something to wrap him in, and get him out of here. Alys, you and Lommie get some water and sponges. We've got to clean up." Melantha moved to d'Branin's side as the others rushed to do as she had told them. "Karoly," she said, putting a gentle hand on his shoulder, "are you all right, Karoly?"

He looked up at her, gray eyes blinking. "I—yes, yes, I am—I told her not to go ahead, Melantha. I told her."

"Yes, you did," Melantha Jhirl said. She gave him a reassuring pat and moved around the table to Agatha Marij-Black. "Agatha," she called. But the psipsych did not respond, not even when Melantha shook her bodily by the shoulders. Her eyes were empty. "She's in shock," Melantha announced. She frowned at the sliver of bone protruding from Marij-Black's cheek. Sponging off her face with a napkin, she carefully removed the splinter.

"What do we do with the body?" asked Lindran. They had found a sheet and wrapped it up. It had finally stopped twitching, although blood continued to seep out, turning the concealing sheet red.

"Put it in a cargo hold," suggested Christopheris.

"No," Melantha said, "not sanitary. It will rot." She thought for a moment. "Suit up and take it down to the driveroom. Cycle it through and lash it in place somehow. Tear up the sheet if you have to. That section of the ship is vacuum. It will be best there."

Christopheris nodded, and the three of them moved off, the deadweight of Lasamer's corpse supported between them. Melantha turned back to Marij-Black, but only for an instant. Lommie Thorne, who was mopping the blood from the tabletop with a piece of cloth, suddenly began to retch violently. Melantha swore. "Someone help her," she snapped.

Karoly d'Branin finally seemed to stir. He rose and took the blood-soaked cloth from Lommie's hand, and led her back to his cabin.

"I can't do this alone," whined Alys Northwind, turning away in disgust.

"Help me, then," Melantha said. Together she and Northwind half-led and half-carried the psipsych from the lounge, cleaned her and undressed her, and put her to sleep with a shot of one of her own drugs. Afterwards Melantha took the injection gun and made the rounds. Northwind and Lommie Thorne required mild tranquilizers, Dannel a somewhat stronger one.

It was three hours before they met again.

* * *

The survivors assembled in the largest of the cargo holds, where three of them hung their sleepwebs. Seven of eight attended. Agatha Marij-Black was still unconscious, sleeping or in a coma or deep shock; none of them were sure. The rest seemed to have recovered, though their faces were pale and drawn. All of them had changed clothes, even Alys Northwind, who had slipped into a new jumpsuit identical to the old one.

"I do not understand," Karoly d'Branin said. "I do not understand what . . ."

"Royd killed him, is all," Northwind said bitterly. "His secret was endangered so he just—just blew him apart. We all saw it."

"I cannot believe that," Karoly d'Branin said in an anguished voice. "I cannot. Royd and I, we have talked, talked many a night when the rest of you were sleeping. He is gentle, inquisitive, sensitive. A dreamer. He understands about the *volcryn.* He would not do such a thing, could not."

"His projection certainly winked out quick enough when it happened," Lindran said. "And you'll notice he hasn't had much to say since."

"The rest of us haven't been unusually talkative either," said Melantha Jhirl. "I don't know what to think, but my impulse is to side with Karoly. We have no proof that the captain was responsible for Thale's death. There's something here none of us understands yet."

Alys Northwind grunted. "Proof," she said disdainfully.

"In fact," Melantha continued, unperturbed, "I'm not even sure *anyone* is responsible. Nothing happened until he was given the esperon. Could the drug be at fault?"

"Hell of a side effect," Lindran muttered.

Rojan Christopheris frowned. "This is not my field, but I would think no. Esperon is extremely potent, with both physical and psionic side effects verging on the extreme, but not *that* extreme."

"What, then?" said Lommie Thorne. "What killed him?"

"The instrument of death was probably his own talent," the xenobiologist said, "undoubtedly augmented by the drug. Besides boosting his principal power, his telepathic sensitivity, esperon would also tend to bring out other psi-talents that might have been latent in him."

"Such as?" Lommie demanded.

"Biocontrol. Telekinesis."

Melantha Jhirl was way ahead of him. "Esperon

shoots blood pressure way up anyway. Increase the pressure in his skull even more by rushing all the blood in his body to his brain. Decrease the air pressure around his head simultaneously, using teke to induce a short-lived vacuum. Think about it."

They thought about it, and none of them liked it.

"Who could do such a thing?" Karoly d'Branin said. "It could only have been self-induced, his own talent wild, out of control."

"Or turned against him by a greater talent," Alys Northwind said stubbornly.

"No human telepath has talent on that order, to seize control of someone else, body and mind and soul, even for an instant."

"Exactly," the stout xenotech replied. "No *human* telepath."

"Gas giant people?" Lommie Thorne's tone was mocking.

Alys Northwind stared her down. "I could talk about Crey sensitives or *githyanki* soulsucks, name a half-dozen others off the top of my head, but I don't need to. I'll only name one. A Hrangan Mind."

That was a disquieting thought. All of them fell silent and stirred uneasily, thinking of the vast, inimical power of a Hrangan Mind hidden in the command chambers of the *Nightflyer*, until Melantha Jhirl broke the spell with a short, derisive laugh. "You're frightening yourself with shadows, Alys," she said. "What you're saying is ridiculous, if you stop to think about it. I hope that isn't too much to ask. You're supposed to be xenologists, the lot of you, experts in alien languages, psychology, biology, technology. You don't act the part. We warred with Old Hranga for a thousand years, but we never communicated successfully with a Hrangan Mind. If Royd Eris is a Hrangan, they've improved their conversational skills markedly in the centuries since the Collapse."

Alys Northwind flushed. "You're right," she said. "I'm jumpy."

"Friends," said Karoly d'Branin, "we must not let our actions be dictated by panic or hysteria. A terrible thing has happened. One of our colleagues is dead, and we do not know why. Until we do, we can only go on. This is no time for rash actions against the innocent. Perhaps, when we return to Avalon, an investigation will tell us what happened. The body is safe for examination, is it not?"

"We cycled it through the airlock into the drive-room," Dannel said. "It'll keep."

"And it can be studied closely on our return," d'Branin said.

"Which should be immediate," said Northwind. "Tell Eris to turn this ship around!"

D'Branin looked stricken. "But the *volcryn*! A week more and we shall know them, if my figures are correct. To return would take us six weeks. Surely it is worth one additional week to know that they exist? Thale would not have wanted his death to be for nothing."

"Before he died, Thale was raving about aliens, about danger," Northwind insisted. "We're rushing to meet some aliens. What if they're the danger? Maybe these *volcryn* are even more potent than a Hrangan Mind, and maybe they don't want to be met, or investigated, or observed. What about that, Karoly? You ever think about that? Those stories of yours—don't some of them talk about terrible things happening to the races that meet the *volcryn*?"

"Legends," d'Branin said. "Superstition."

"A whole Fyndii horde vanishes in one legend," Rojan Christopheris put in.

"We cannot put credence in these fears of others," d'Branin argued.

"Perhaps there's nothing to the stories," Northwind

said, "but do you care to risk it? *I* don't. For what? Your sources may be fictional or exaggerated or wrong, your interpretations and computations may be in error, or they may have changed course—the *volcryn* may not even be within light-years of where we'll drop out."

"Ah," Melantha Jhirl said, "I understand. Then we shouldn't go on because they won't be there, and besides, they might be dangerous."

D'Branin smiled and Lindran laughed. "Not funny," protested Alys Northwind, but she argued no further.

"No," Melantha continued, "any danger we are in will not increase significantly in the time it will take us to drop out of drive and look about for the *volcryn*. We have to drop out anyway, to reprogram for the shunt home. Besides, we've come a long way for these *volcryn*, and I admit to being curious." She looked at each of them in turn, but no one spoke. "We continue, then."

"And Royd?" demanded Christopheris. "What do we do about him?"

"What *can* we do?" said Dannel.

"Treat the captain as before," Melantha said decisively. "We should open lines to him and talk. Maybe now we can clear up some of the mysteries that are bothering us, if Royd is willing to discuss things frankly."

"He is probably as shocked and dismayed as we are,

my friends," said d'Branin. "Possibly he is fearful that we will blame him, try to hurt him."

"I think we should cut through to his section of the ship and drag him out kicking and screaming," Christopheris said. "We have the tools. That would write a quick end to all our fears."

"It could kill Royd," Melantha said. "Then he'd be justified in anything he did to stop us. He controls this ship. He could do a great deal, if he decided we were his enemies." She shook her head vehemently. "No, Rojan, we can't attack Royd. We've got to reassure him. I'll do it, if no one else wants to talk to him." There were no volunteers. "All right. But I don't want any of you trying any foolish schemes. Go about your business. Act normally."

Karoly d'Branin was nodding agreement. "Let us put Royd and poor Thale from our minds, and concern ourselves with our work, with our preparations. Our sensory instruments must be ready for deployment as soon as we shift out of drive and reenter normal space, so we can find our quarry quickly. We must review everything we know of the *volcryn*." He turned to the linguists and began discussing some of the preliminaries he expected of them, and in a short time the talk had turned to the *volcryn,* and bit by bit the fear drained out of the group.

Lommie Thorne sat listening quietly, her thumb absently rubbing her wrist implant, but no one noticed the thoughtful look in her eyes.

Not even Royd Eris, watching.

Melantha Jhirl returned to the lounge alone.

Someone had turned out the lights. "Captain?" she said softly.

He appeared to her; pale, glowing softly, with eyes that did not see. His clothes, filmy and out-of-date, were all shades of white and faded blue. "Hello, Melantha," the mellow voice said from the communicators, as the ghost silently mouthed the same words.

"Did you hear, captain?"

"Yes," he said, his voice vaguely tinged by surprise. "I hear and I see everything on my *Nightflyer,* Melantha. Not only in the lounge, and not only when the communicators and viewscreens are on. How long have you known?"

"Known?" She smiled. "Since you praised Alys's gas giant solution to the Roydian mystery. The communicators were not on that night. You had no way of knowing. Unless . . ."

"I have never made a mistake before," Royd said. "I

told Karoly, but that was deliberate. I am sorry. I have been under stress."

"I believe you, captain," she said. "No matter. I'm the improved model, remember? I'd guessed weeks ago."

For a time Royd said nothing. Then: "When do you begin to reassure me?"

"I'm doing so right now. Don't you feel reassured yet?"

The apparition gave a ghostly shrug. "I am pleased that you and Karoly do not think I murdered that man. Otherwise, I am frightened. Things are getting out of control, Melantha. Why didn't she listen to me? I told Karoly to keep him dampened. I told Agatha not to give him that injection. I warned them."

"They were afraid, too," Melantha said. "Afraid that you were only trying to frighten them off, to protect some awful plan. I don't know. It was my fault, in a sense. I was the one who suggested esperon. I thought it would put Thale at ease, and tell us something about you. I was curious." She frowned. "A deadly curiosity. Now I have blood on my hands."

Melantha's eyes were adjusting to the darkness in the lounge. By the faint light of the holograph, she could see the table where it had happened, dark streaks of drying blood across its surface among the plates and cups and cold pots of tea and chocolate. She heard a faint dripping as well, and could not tell if it was blood or coffee. She shivered. "I don't like it in here."

"If you would like to leave, I can be with you wherever you go."

"No," she said. "I'll stay. Royd, I think it might be better if you were *not* with us wherever we go. If you kept silent and out of sight, so to speak. If I asked you to, would you shut off your monitors throughout the ship? Except for the lounge, perhaps. It would make the others feel better, I'm sure."

"They don't know."

"They will. You made that remark about gas giants in everyone's hearing. Some of them have probably figured it out by now."

"If I told you I had cut myself off, you would have no way of knowing whether it was the truth."

"I could trust you," Melantha Jhirl said.

Silence. The spectre stared at her. "As you wish," Royd's voice said finally. "Everything off. Now I see and hear only in here. Now, Melantha, you must promise to control them. No secret schemes, or attempts to breach my quarters. Can you do that?"

"I think so," she said.

"Did you believe my story?" Royd asked.

"Ah," she said. "A strange and wondrous story, captain. If it's a lie, I'll swap lies with you anytime. You do it well. If it's true, then you are a strange and wondrous man."

"It's true," the ghost said quietly. "Melantha . . ."

"Yes?"

"Does it bother you that I have . . . watched you? Watched you when you were not aware?"

"A little," she said, "but I think I can understand it."

"I watched you copulating."

She smiled. "Ah," she said, "I'm good at it."

"I wouldn't know," Royd said. "You're good to watch."

Silence. She tried not to hear the steady, faint dripping off to her right. "Yes," she said after a long hesitation.

"Yes? What?"

"Yes, Royd," she said, "I would probably sex with you if it were possible."

"How did you know what I was thinking?" Royd's voice was suddenly frightened, full of anxiety and something close to fear.

"Easy," Melantha said, startled. "I'm an improved model. It wasn't so difficult to figure out. I told you, remember? I'm three moves ahead of you."

"You're not a telepath, are you?"

"No," Melantha said. "No."

Royd considered that for a long time. "I believe I'm reassured," he said at last.

"Good," she said.

"Melantha," he added, "one thing. Sometimes it is not wise to be too many moves ahead. Do you understand?"

"Oh? No, not really. You frighten me. Now reassure me. Your turn, Captain Royd."

"Of what?"

"What happened in here? Really?"

Royd said nothing.

"I think you know something," Melantha said. "You gave up your secret to stop us from injecting Lasamer with esperon. Even after your secret was forfeit, you ordered us not to go ahead. Why?"

"Esperon is a dangerous drug," Royd said.

"More than that, captain," Melantha said. "You're evading. What killed Thale Lasamer? Or is it *who*?"

"*I* didn't."

"One of us? The *volcryn*?"

Royd said nothing.

"Is there an alien aboard your ship, captain?"

Silence.

"Are we in danger? Am *I* in danger, captain? I'm not afraid. Does that make me a fool?"

"I like people," Royd said at last. "When I can stand it, I like to have passengers. I watch them, yes. It's not so terrible. I like you and Karoly especially. I won't let anything happen to you."

"What might happen?"

Royd said nothing.

"And what about the others, Royd? Christopheris and Northwind, Dannel and Lindran, Lommie Thorne? Are you taking care of them, too? Or only Karoly and I?"

No reply.

"You're not very talkative tonight," Melantha observed.

"I'm under strain," his voice replied. "And certain things you are safer not to know. Go to bed, Melantha Jhirl. We've talked long enough."

"All right, captain," she said. She smiled at the ghost and lifted her hand. His own rose to meet it. Warm dark flesh and pale radiance brushed, melded, were one.

Melantha Jhirl turned to go. It was not until she was out in the corridor, safe in the light once more, that she began to tremble.

False midnight.

The talks had broken up, and one by one the academicians had gone to bed. Even Karoly d'Branin had retired, his appetite for chocolate quelled by his memories of the lounge.

The linguists had made violent, noisy love before giving themselves up to sleep, as if to reaffirm their life in the face of Thale Lasamer's grisly death. Rojan Christopheris had listened to music. But now they were all still.

The *Nightflyer* was filled with silence.

In the darkness of the largest cargo hold, three sleepwebs hung side by side. Melantha Jhirl twisted occasionally in her sleep, her face feverish, as if in the grip of some nightmare. Alys Northwind lay flat on her back, snoring loudly, a reassuring wheeze of noise from her solid, meaty chest.

Lommie Thorne lay awake, thinking.

Finally she rose and dropped to the floor, nude, quiet, light and careful as a cat. She pulled on a tight pair of pants, slipped a wide-sleeved shirt of black metallic cloth over her head, belted it with a silver chain, shook out her short hair. She did not don her boots. Barefoot was quieter. Her feet were small and soft, with no trace of callouses.

She moved to the middle sleepweb and shook Alys Northwind by her shoulder. The snoring stopped abruptly.

"Huh?" the xenotech said. She grunted in annoyance.

"Come," whispered Lommie Thorne. She beckoned.

Northwind got heavily to her feet, blinking, and followed the cyberneticist through the door, out into the corridor. She'd been sleeping in her jumpsuit, its seam open nearly to her crotch. She frowned and sealed it. "What the hell," she muttered. She was disarrayed and unhappy.

"There's a way to find out if Royd's story was true," Lommie Thorne said carefully. "Melantha won't like it, though. Are you game to try?"

"What?" Northwind asked. Her face betrayed her interest.

"Come," the cyberneticist said.

They moved silently through the ship, to the computer room. The system was up, but dormant. They entered quietly; all empty. Currents of light ran silkily down crystalline channels in the data grids, meeting, joining, splitting apart again; rivers of wan multihued radiance crisscrossing a black landscape. The chamber was dim, the only noise a buzz at the edge of human hearing, until Lommie Thorne moved through it, touching keys, tripping switches, directing the silent luminescent currents. Bit by bit the machine woke.

"What are you *doing*?" Alys Northwind said.

"Karoly told me to tie in our system with the ship," Lommie Thorne replied as she worked. "I was told Royd wanted to study the *volcryn* data. Fine, I did it. Do you understand what that means?" Her shirt whispered in soft metallic tones when she moved.

Eagerness broke across the flat features of xenotech Alys Northwind. "The two systems are tied together!"

"Exactly. So Royd can find out about the *volcryn,* and we can find out about Royd." She frowned. "I wish I knew more about the *Nightflyer*'s hardware, but I think I can feel my way through. This is a pretty sophisticated system d'Branin requisitioned."

"Can you take over from Eris?"

"Take over?" Lommie sounded puzzled. "You been drinking again, Alys?"

"No, I'm serious. Use your system to break into the ship's control, overwhelm Eris, countermand his orders, make the *Nightflyer* respond to us, down here. Wouldn't you feel safer if we were in control?"

"Maybe," the cyberneticist said doubtfully. "I could try, but why do that?"

"Just in case. We don't have to use the capacity. Just so we have it, if an emergency arises."

Lommie Thorne shrugged. "Emergencies and gas giants. I only want to put my mind at rest about Royd, whether he had anything to do with killing Lasamer." She moved over to a readout panel, where a half-dozen meter-square viewscreens curved around a console, and brought one of them to life. Long fingers ghosted through holographic keys that appeared and disappeared as she used them, the keyboard changing shape again and yet again. The cyberneticist's pretty face grew thoughtful and serious. "We're in," she said. Characters began to flow across a viewscreen, red flickerings in glassy black depths. On a second screen, a schematic of the *Nightflyer* appeared, revolved, halved; its spheres shifted size and perspective at the whim of Lommie's fingers, and a line of numerals below gave the specifications. The cyberneticist watched, and finally froze both screens.

"Here," she said, "here's my answer about the hardware. You can dismiss your takeover idea, unless those gas giant people of yours are going to help. The *Night-flyer*'s bigger and smarter than our little system here. Makes sense, when you stop to think about it. Ship's all automated, except for Royd."

Her hands moved again, and two more display screens stirred. Lommie Thorne whistled and coaxed her search program with soft words of encouragement. "It looks as though there *is* a Royd, though. Configurations are all wrong for a robot ship. Damn, I would have bet anything." The characters began to flow again, Lommie watching the figures as they drifted by. "Here's life support specs, might tell us something." A finger jabbed, and one screen froze yet again.

"Nothing unusual," Alys Northwind said in disappointment.

"Standard waste disposal. Water recycling. Food processor, with protein and vitamin supplements in stores." She began to whistle. "Tanks of Renny's moss and neograss to eat up the CO_2. Oxygen cycle, then. No methane or ammonia. Sorry about that."

"Go sex with a computer!"

The cyberneticist smiled. "Ever tried it?" Her fingers moved again. "What else should I look for? You're the tech, what would be a giveaway? Give me some ideas."

"Check the specs for nurturant tanks, cloning

equipment, that sort of thing," the xenotech said. "That would tell us whether he was lying."

"I don't know," Lommie Thorne said. "Long time ago. He might have junked that stuff. No use for it."

"Find Royd's life history," Northwind said. "His mother's. Get a readout on the business they've done, all this alleged trading. They must have records. Account books, profit-and-loss, cargo invoices, that kind of thing." Her voice grew excited, and she gripped the cyberneticist from behind by her shoulders. "A log, a ship's log! There's got to be a log. Find it!"

"All right." Lommie Thorne whistled, happy, at ease with her system, riding the data winds, curious, in control. Then the screen in front of her turned a bright red and began to blink. She smiled, touched a ghost key, and the keyboard melted away and re-formed under her. She tried another tack. Three more screens turned red and began to blink. Her smile faded.

"What is it?"

"Security," said Lommie Thorne. "I'll get through it in a second. Hold on." She changed the keyboard yet again, entered another search program, attached on a rider in case it was blocked. Another screen flashed red. She had her machine chew the data she'd gathered, sent out another feeler. More red. Flashing. Blinking. Bright enough to hurt the eyes. All the screens were red now. "A good security program," she said with admiration. "The log is well protected."

Alys Northwind grunted. "Are we blocked?"

"Response time is too slow," Lommie Thorne said, chewing on her lower lip as she thought. "There's a way to fix that." She smiled, and rolled back the soft black metal of her sleeve.

"What are you doing?"

"Watch," she said. She slid her arm under the console, found the prongs, jacked in.

"Ah," she said, low in her throat. The flashing red blocks vanished from her readout screens, one after the other, as she sent her mind coursing into the *Nightflyer*'s system, easing through all the blocks. "Nothing like slipping past another system's security. Like slipping onto a man." Log entries were flickering past them in a whirling, blurring rush, too fast for Alys Northwind to read. But Lommie read them.

Then she stiffened. "Oh," she said. It was almost a whimper. "Cold," she said. She shook her head and it was gone, but there was a sound in her ears, a terrible whooping sound. "Damn," she said, "that'll wake everyone." She glanced up when she felt Alys's fingers dig painfully into her shoulder, squeezing, hurting.

A gray steel panel slid almost silently across the access to the corridor, cutting off the whooping cry of the alarm. "What?" Lommie Thorne said.

"That's an emergency airseal," said Alys Northwind in a dead voice. She knew starships. "It closes where they're about to load or unload cargo in vacuum."

Their eyes went to the huge, curving, outer airlock above their heads. The inner lock was almost completely open, and as they watched it clicked into place, and the seal on the outer door cracked, and now it was open half a meter, sliding, and beyond was twisted nothingness so burning-bright it seared the eyes.

"Oh," said Lommie Thorne, as the cold coursed up her arm. She had stopped whistling.

Alarms were hooting everywhere. The passengers began to stir. Melantha Jhirl tumbled from her sleepweb and darted into the corridor, nude, frantic, alert. Karoly d'Branin sat up drowsily. The psipsych muttered fitfully in drug-induced sleep. Rojan Christopheris cried out in alarm.

Far away, metal crunched and tore, and a violent shudder ran through the ship, throwing the linguists out of their sleepwebs, knocking Melantha from her feet.

In the command quarters of the *Nightflyer* was a spherical room with featureless white walls, a lesser sphere—a suspended control console—floating in its center. The walls were always blank when the ship was in drive; the warped and glaring underside of spacetime was painful to behold.

But now darkness woke in the room, a holoscope coming to life, cold black and stars everywhere, points of icy unwinking brilliance, no up and no down and no direction, the floating control sphere the only feature in the simulated sea of night.

The *Nightflyer* had shifted out of drive.

Melantha Jhirl found her feet again and thumbed on a communicator. The alarms were still hooting, and it was hard to hear. "Captain," she shouted, "what's happening?"

"I don't know," Royd's voice replied. "I'm trying to find out. Wait."

Melantha waited. Karoly d'Branin came staggering out into the corridor, blinking and rubbing his eyes. Rojan Christopheris was not long behind him. "What is it? What's wrong?" he demanded, but Melantha just shook her head. Lindran and Dannel soon appeared as well. There was no sign of Marij-Black, Alys Northwind, or Lommie Thorne. The academicians looked uneasily at the seal that blocked cargo hold three.

Finally Melantha told Christopheris to go look. He returned a few minutes later. "Agatha is still unconscious," he said, talking at the top of his voice to be heard over the alarms. "The drugs still have her. She's moving around, though. Crying out."

"Alys and Lommie?"

Christopheris shrugged. "I can't find them. Ask your friend Royd."

The communicator came back to life as the alarms died. "We have returned to normal space," Royd's voice said, "but the ship is damaged. Hold three, your computer room, was breached while we were under drive. It was ripped apart by the flux. The computer dropped us out of drive automatically, fortunately for us, or the drive forces might have torn my entire ship apart."

"Royd," said Melantha, "Northwind and Thorne are missing."

"It appears your computer was in use when the hold was breached," Royd said carefully. "I would presume them dead, although I cannot say that with certainty. At Melantha's request I have deactivated most of my monitors, retaining only the lounge input. I do not know what transpired. But this is a small ship, and if they are not with you, we must assume the worst." He paused briefly. "If it is any consolation, they died swiftly and painlessly."

"You killed them," Christopheris said, his face red and angry. He started to say more, but Melantha slipped her hand firmly over his mouth. The two linguists exchanged a long, meaningful look.

"Do we know how it happened, captain?" Melantha asked.

"Yes," he said, reluctantly.

The xenobiologist had taken the hint, and Melantha took away her hand to let him breathe. "Royd?" she prompted.

"It sounds insane, Melantha," his voice replied, "but it appears your colleagues opened the hold's loading lock. I doubt they did so deliberately, of course. They were using the system interface to gain entry to the *Nightflyer*'s data storage and controls, and they shunted aside all the safeties."

"I see," Melantha said. "A terrible tragedy."

"Yes. Perhaps more terrible than you think. I have yet to discover the extent of damage to my ship."

"We should not keep you if you have duties to perform," Melantha said. "All of us are shocked, and it is difficult to talk now. Investigate the condition of your ship, and we'll continue our discussion at a more opportune time. Agreed?"

"Yes," said Royd.

Melantha turned off the communicator. Now, in theory, the device was dead; Royd could neither see nor hear them.

"Do you believe him?" Christopheris snapped.

"I don't know," Melantha Jhirl said, "but I do know that the other cargo holds can all be flushed just as hold three was. I'm moving my sleepweb into a cabin. I suggest that those of you who are living in hold two do the same."

"Clever," Lindran said, with a sharp nod of her head. "We can crowd in. It won't be comfortable, but I doubt that I'd sleep the sleep of angels in the holds after this."

"We should also get our suits out of storage in four," Dannel suggested. "Keep them close at hand. Just in case."

"If you wish," Melantha said. "It's possible that all the locks might pop open simultaneously. Royd can't fault us for taking precautions." She flashed a grim smile. "After today we've earned the right to act irrationally."

"This is no time for your damned jokes, Melantha,"

Christopheris said. He was still red-faced, and his tone was full of fear and anger. "Three people are dead, Agatha is perhaps deranged or catatonic, the rest of us are endangered—"

"Yes. And we still have no idea what is happening," Melantha pointed out.

"Royd Eris is killing us!" Christopheris shrieked. "I don't know who or what he is and I don't know if that story he gave us is true and I don't *care.* Maybe he's a Hrangan Mind or the avenging angel of the *volcryn* or the second coming of Jesus Christ. What the hell difference does it make? He's *killing* us!" He looked at each of them in turn. "Any one of us could be next," he added. "Any one of us. Unless . . . we've got to make plans, *do* something, put a stop to this once and for all."

"You realize," Melantha said gently, "that we cannot actually know whether the good captain has turned off his sensory inputs down here. He could be watching and listening to us right now. He isn't, of course. He said he wouldn't and I believe him. But we have only his word on that. Now, Rojan, you don't appear to trust Royd. If that's so, you can hardly put any faith in his promises. It follows, therefore, that from your own point of view it might not be wise to say the things that you're saying." She smiled slyly. "Do you understand the implications of what I'm saying?"

Christopheris opened his mouth and closed it again, looking very like a tall, ugly fish. He said nothing, but his eyes moved furtively, and his flush deepened.

Lindran smiled thinly. "I think he's got it," she said.

"The computer is gone, then," Karoly d'Branin said suddenly in a low voice.

Melantha looked at him. "I'm afraid so, Karoly."

D'Branin ran his fingers through his hair, as if half aware of how untidy he looked. "The *volcryn,*" he muttered. "How will we work without the computer?" He nodded to himself. "I have a small unit in my cabin, a wrist model, perhaps it will suffice. It *must* suffice, it must. I will get the figures from Royd, learn where we have dropped out. Excuse me, my friends. Pardon, I must go." He wandered away in a distracted haze, talking to himself.

"He hasn't heard a word we've said," Dannel said, incredulous.

"Think how distraught he'd be if *all* of us were dead," added Lindran. "Then he'd have no one to help him look for the *volcryn.*"

"Let him go," Melantha said. "He is as hurt as any of

us, maybe more so. He wears it differently. His obsessions are his defense."

"Ah. And what is *our* defense?"

"Patience, maybe," said Melantha Jhirl. "All of the dead were trying to breach Royd's secret when they died. We haven't tried. Here we are discussing their deaths."

"You don't find that suspicious?" asked Lindran.

"Very," Melantha said. "I even have a method of testing my suspicions. One of us can make yet another attempt to find out whether our captain told us the truth. If he or she dies, we'll know." She shrugged. "Forgive me, however, if I'm not the one who tries. But don't let me stop you if you have the urge. I'll note the results with interest. Until then, I'm going to move out of the cargo hold and get some sleep." She turned and strode off, leaving the others to stare at one another.

"Arrogant bitch," Dannel observed almost conversationally after Melantha had left.

"Do you really think he can hear us?" Christopheris whispered to the two linguists.

"Every pithy word," Lindran said. She smiled at his discomfiture. "Come, Dannel, let's get to a safe area and back to bed."

He nodded.

"But," said Christopheris, "we have to *do* something. Make plans. Defenses."

Lindran gave him a final withering look, and pulled Dannel off behind her down the corridor.

"Melantha? Karoly?"

She woke quickly, alert at the mere whisper of her name, fully awake almost at once, and sat up in the narrow single bed. Squeezed in beside her, Karoly d'Branin groaned and rolled over, yawning.

"Royd?" she asked. "Is it morning?"

"We are drifting in interstellar space three light-years from the nearest star, Melantha," replied the soft voice from the walls. "In such a context, the term *morning* has no meaning. But, yes, it is morning."

Melantha laughed. "*Drifting,* you said? How bad is the damage?"

"Serious, but not dangerous. Hold three is a complete ruin, hanging from my ship like half of a broken egg, but the damage was confined. The drives themselves are intact, and the *Nightflyer*'s computers did not seem to suffer from your system's destruction. I feared they might. I have heard of phenomena like electronic death traumas."

D'Branin said, "Eh? Royd?"

Melantha stroked him affectionately. "I'll tell you later, Karoly," she said. "Go back to sleep. Royd, you sound serious. Is there more?"

"I am worried about our return flight, Melantha," Royd said. "When I take the *Nightflyer* back into drive, the flux will be playing directly on portions of the ship that were never engineered to withstand it. Our configurations are askew now; I can show you the mathematics of it, but the question of the flux forces is the vital one. The airseal across the access to hold three is a particular concern. I've run some simulations, and I don't know if it can take the stress. If it bursts, my whole ship will split apart in the middle. My engines will go shunting off by themselves, and the rest—even if the life support sphere remains intact, we will all soon be dead."

"I see. Is there anything we can do?"

"Yes. The exposed areas would be easy enough to reinforce. The outer hull is armored to withstand the warping forces, of course. We could mount it in place, a crude shield, but according to my projections it would suffice. If we do it correctly, it will help correct our configurations as well. Large portions of the hull were torn loose when the locks opened, but they are still out there, most within a kilometer or two, and could be used."

At some point Karoly d'Branin had finally come awake. "My team has four vacuum sleds," he said. "We can retrieve those pieces for you, my friend."

"Fine, Karoly, but that is not my primary concern. My ship is self-repairing within certain limits, but this exceeds those limits by an order of magnitude. I will have to do this myself."

"You?" D'Branin was startled. "Royd, you said—that is, your muscles, your weakness—this work will be too much for you. Surely we can do this for you!"

Royd's reply was tolerant. "I am only a cripple in a gravity field, Karoly. Weightless, I am in my element, and I will be killing the *Nightflyer*'s gravity grid momentarily, to try to gather my own strength for the repair work. No, you misunderstand. I am capable of the work. I have the tools, including my own heavy-duty sled."

"I think I know what you are concerned about, captain," Melantha said.

"I'm glad," Royd said. "Perhaps then you can answer my question. If I emerge from the safety of my chambers to do this work, can you keep your colleagues from harming me?"

Karoly d'Branin was shocked. "Oh, Royd, Royd, how could you think such a thing? We are scholars, scientists, not—not criminals, or soldiers, or—or animals, we are human, how can you believe we would threaten you or do you harm?"

"Human," Royd repeated, "but alien to me, suspicious of me. Give me no false assurances, Karoly."

He sputtered. Melantha took him by the hand and bid him quiet. "Royd," she said, "I won't lie to you. You'd be in some danger. But I'd hope that, by coming out, you'd make our friends joyously happy. They'd be able to see that you told the truth, see that you were only human." She smiled. "They *would* see that, wouldn't they?"

"They would," Royd said, "but would it be enough to offset their suspicions? They believe I am responsible for the deaths of the other three, do they not?"

"Believe is too strong a word. They suspect it, they fear it. They are frightened, captain, and with good cause. *I* am frightened."

"No more than I."

"I would be less frightened if I knew what *did* happen. Will you tell me?"

Silence.

"Royd, if—"

"I have made mistakes, Melantha," Royd said gravely. "But I am not alone in that. I did my best to stop the esperon injection, and I failed. I might have saved Alys and Lommie if I had seen them, heard them, known what they were about. But you made me turn off my monitors, Melantha. I cannot help what I cannot see. Why, if you saw three moves ahead, did you not calculate these results?"

Melantha Jhirl felt briefly guilty. "*Mea culpa*, captain, I share the blame. I know that. Believe me, I know that. It is hard to see three moves ahead when you do not know the rules, however. Tell me the rules."

"I am blind and deaf," Royd said, ignoring her. "It is frustrating. I cannot help if I am blind and deaf. I am going to turn on the monitors again, Melantha. I am sorry if you do not approve. I want your approval, but I must do this with or without it. I have to see."

"Turn them on," Melantha said thoughtfully. "I was wrong, captain. I should never have asked you to blind yourself. I did not understand the situation, and I overestimated my own power to control the others. A failing of mine. Improved models too often think they can do anything." Her mind was racing, and she felt almost sick; she had miscalculated, misled, and there was more blood on her hands. "I think I understand better now."

"Understand what?" Karoly d'Branin said, baffled.

"You do *not* understand," Royd said sternly. "Don't pretend that you do, Melantha Jhirl. Don't! It is not wise or safe to be too many moves ahead." There was something disturbing in his tone.

Melantha understood that, too.

"What?" Karoly said. "I do not understand."

"Neither do I," Melantha said carefully. "Neither do I, Karoly." She kissed him lightly. "None of us understands, do we?"

"Good," said Royd.

She nodded, and put a reassuring arm around Karoly. "Royd," she said, "to return to the question of repairs, it seems to me you must do this work, regardless of what promises we can give you. You won't risk your ship by slipping back into drive in your present condition, and the only other option is to drift out here until we all die. What choice do we have?"

"I have a choice," Royd said with deadly seriousness. "I could kill all of you, if that were the only way to save myself and my ship."

"You could try," Melantha said.

"Let us have no more talk of death," d'Branin said.

"You are right, Karoly," Royd said, "I do not wish to kill any of you. But I must be protected."

"You will be," Melantha said. "Karoly can set the others to chasing your hull fragments. I'll be your protection. I'll stay by your side. If anyone tries to attack you, they'll have to deal with me. They won't find that easy. And I can assist you. The work will be done three times as fast."

Royd was polite. "It is my experience that most planet-born are clumsy and easily tired in weightlessness. It would be more efficient if I worked alone, although I will gladly accept your services as a bodyguard."

"I remind you that I'm the improved model, captain," Melantha said. "Good in free fall as well as in bed. I'll help."

"You are stubborn. As you will, then. In a few moments I shall depower the gravity grid. Karoly, go and prepare your people. Unship your vacuum sleds and suit up. I will exit the *Nightflyer* in three standard hours, after I have recovered from the pains of your gravity. I want all of you outside the ship before I leave. Is that condition understood?"

"Yes," said Karoly. "All except Agatha. She has not regained consciousness, friend, she will not be a problem."

"No," said Royd, "I meant *all* of you, including Agatha. Take her outside with you."

"But Royd!" protested d'Branin.

"You're the captain," Melantha Jhirl said firmly. "It will be as you say; all of us outside. Including Agatha."

* * *

Outside. It was as though some vast animal had taken a bite out of the stars.

Melantha Jhirl waited on her sled close by the *Nightflyer* and looked at the stars. It was not so very different out here in the depths of interstellar space. The stars were cold, frozen points of light; unwinking, austere, more chill and uncaring somehow than the same suns made to dance and twinkle by an atmosphere. Only the absence of a landmark primary reminded her of where she was: in the places between, where men and women and their ships do not stop, where the *volcryn* sail crafts impossibly ancient. She tried to pick out Avalon's sun, but she did not know where to search. The configurations were strange to her and she had no idea of how she was oriented. Behind her, before her, above, all around, the starfields stretched endlessly. She glanced down, or what seemed like down just then, beyond her feet and her sled and the *Nightflyer,* expecting still more alien stars. And the *bite* hit her with an almost physical force.

Melantha fought off a wave of vertigo. She was suspended above a pit, a yawning chasm in the universe, black, starless, vast.

Empty.

She remembered then: the Tempter's Veil. Just a cloud

of dark gases, nothing really, galactic pollution that obscured the light from the stars of the Fringe. But this close at hand, it seemed immense, terrifying, and she had to break her gaze when she began to feel as if she were falling. It was a gulf beneath her and the frail silver-white shell of the *Nightflyer,* a gulf about to swallow them.

Melantha touched one of the controls on the sled's forked handle, swinging around so the Veil was to her side instead of beneath her. That seemed to help somehow. She concentrated on the *Nightflyer,* ignoring the looming wall of blackness beyond. It was the largest object in her universe, bright amid the darkness, ungainly, its shattered cargo sphere giving the whole craft an unbalanced cast.

She could see the other sleds as they angled through the black, tracking the missing pieces of hull, grappling with them, bringing them back. The linguistic team worked together, as always, sharing a sled. Rojan Christopheris was alone, working in a sullen silence. Melantha had almost had to threaten him with physical violence before he agreed to join them. The xenobiologist was certain that it was all another plot, that once they were outside, the *Nightflyer* would slip into drive without them and leave them to lingering deaths.

His suspicions were inflamed by drink, and there had been alcohol on his breath when Melantha and Karoly had finally forced him to suit up. Karoly had a sled too, and a silent passenger; Agatha Marij-Black, freshly drugged and asleep in her vacuum suit, safely locked into place.

While her colleagues labored, Melantha Jhirl waited for Royd Eris, talking to the others occasionally over the comm link. The two linguists, unaccustomed to weightlessness, were complaining a good deal, and bickering as well. Karoly tried to soothe them frequently. Christopheris said little, and his few comments were edged and biting. He was still angry. Melantha watched him flit across her field of vision, a stick figure in formfitting black armor, standing erect at the controls of his sled.

Finally the circular airlock atop the foremost of the *Nightflyer*'s major spheres dilated and Royd Eris emerged.

She watched him approach, curious, wondering what he would look like. In her mind were a half-dozen contradictory pictures. His genteel, cultured, too-formal voice sometimes reminded her of the dark aristocrats of her native Prometheus, the wizards who toyed with human genes and played baroque status games. At other times his naïveté made her imagine him as an inexperienced youth. His ghost was a tired-looking thin young man, and he was supposed to be considerably older than that pale shadow, but Melantha found it difficult to hear an old man talking when he spoke.

Melantha felt a nervous tingle as he neared. The lines of his sled and his suit were different from theirs, disturbingly so. Alien, she thought, and quickly squelched the thought. Such differences meant nothing. Royd's sled was large, a long oval plate with eight jointed grappling arms bristling from its underside like the legs of a metallic spider. A heavy-duty cutting laser was mounted beneath the controls, its snout jutting threateningly forward. His suit was far more massive than the carefully engineered Academy worksuits they wore, with a bulge between its shoulder blades that was probably a power pack, and rakish radiant fins atop shoulders and helmet. It made him seem hulking, hunched and deformed.

But when he finally came near enough for Melantha to see his face, it was just a face.

White, very white, that was the predominant impression she got; white hair cropped very short, a white stubble around the sharply chiseled lines of his jaw, almost invisible eyebrows beneath which his eyes moved restlessly. His eyes were large and vividly blue, his best feature. His skin was pale and unlined, scarcely touched by time.

He looked wary, she thought. And perhaps a bit frightened.

Royd stopped his sled close to hers, amid the twisted ruin that had been cargo hold three, and surveyed the damage, the pieces of floating wreckage that had once been flesh, blood, glass, metal, plastic. Hard to distinguish now, all of them fused and burned and frozen together. "We have a good deal of work to do," he said. "Shall we begin?"

"First let's talk," she replied. She shifted her sled closer and reached out to him, but the distance was still too great, the width of the bases of the two vacuum sleds keeping them apart. Melantha backed off and turned herself over completely, so that Royd stood upside down in her world and she upside down in his. She moved to him again, positioning her sled directly over/under his. Their gloved hands met, brushed, parted. Melantha adjusted her altitude. Their helmets touched.

"Now I have touched you," Royd said, with a tremor in his voice. "I have never touched anyone before, or been touched."

"Oh, Royd. This isn't touching, not really. The suits are in the way. But I will touch you, *really* touch you. I promise you that."

"You can't. It's impossible."

"I'll find a way," she said firmly. "Now, turn off your comm. The sound will carry through our helmets."

He blinked and used his tongue controls and it was done. "Now we can talk," she said. "Privately."

"I do not like this, Melantha," he said. "This is too obvious. This is dangerous."

"There is no other way. Royd, I *do* know."

"Yes," he said. "I knew you did. Three moves ahead, Melantha. I remember the way you play chess. But this is a more serious game, and you are safer if you feign ignorance."

"I understand that, captain. Other things I'm less sure about. Can we talk about them?"

"No. Don't ask me to. Just do as I tell you. You are in peril, all of you, but I can protect you. The less you know, the better I can protect you." Through the transparent faceplates, his expression was somber.

She stared into his upside-down eyes. "It might be a second crew member, someone else hidden in your quarters, but I don't believe that. It's the ship, isn't it? Your ship is killing us. Not you. It. Only that doesn't make sense. You command the *Nightflyer*. How can it act independently? And why? What motive? And how was Thale Lasamer killed? The business with Alys and Lommie, that was easy, but a psionic murder? A starship with psi? I can't accept that. It can't be the ship. Yet it can't be anything else. Help me, captain."

He blinked, anguish behind his eyes. "I should never have accepted Karoly's charter, not with a telepath among you. It was too risky. But I wanted to see the *volcryn,* and he spoke of them so movingly." He sighed. "You understand too much already, Melantha. I can't tell you more, or I would be powerless to protect you. The ship is malfunctioning, that is all you need to know. It is not safe to push too hard. As long as I am at the controls, I think I can keep you and the others from harm. Trust me."

"Trust is a two-way bond," Melantha said.

Royd lifted his hand and pushed her away, then tongued his communicator back to life. "Enough gossip," he announced. "We have work to do. Come. I want to see just how improved you actually are."

In the solitude of her helmet, Melantha Jhirl swore softly.

With an irregular twist of metal locked beneath him in his sled's magnetic grip, Rojan Christopheris sailed back towards the *Nightflyer.* He was watching from a distance when Royd Eris emerged on his oversized work sled. He was closer when Melantha Jhirl moved to him, inverted her sled, and pressed her faceplate to Royd's. Christopheris listened to their soft exchange, heard Melantha promise to touch him, Eris, the *thing,* the killer. He swallowed his rage. Then they cut him out, cut all of them out, went off the open circuit. But still she hung there, suspended by that cipher in the hunchbacked spacesuit, faces pressed together like two lovers kissing.

Christopheris swept in close, unlocked his captive plate so it would drift towards them. "Here," he announced. "I'm off to get another." He tongued off his own comm and swore, and his sled slid around the spheres and tubes of the *Nightflyer.*

Somehow they were all in it together, Royd and Melantha and possibly old d'Branin as well, he thought sourly. She had protected Eris from the first, stopped them when they might have taken action together, found out who or what he was. He did not trust her. His skin crawled when he remembered that they had been to bed together. She and Eris were the same, whatever they might be. And now poor Alys was dead, and that fool Thorne and even that damned telepath, but still Melantha was with him, against them. Rojan Christopheris was deeply afraid, and angry, and half drunk.

The others were out of sight, off chasing spinning wedges of half-slagged metal. Royd and Melantha were engrossed in each other, the ship abandoned and vulnerable. This was his chance. No wonder Eris had insisted that all of them precede him into the void; outside, isolated from the controls of the *Nightflyer,* he was only a man. A weak one at that.

Smiling a thin, hard smile, Christopheris brought his sled curling around the cargo spheres, hidden from sight, and vanished into the gaping maw of the drive-room. It was a long tunnel, everything open to vacuum, safe from the corrosion of an atmosphere. Like most starships, the *Nightflyer* had a triple propulsion system: the gravfield for landing and lifting, useless away from a gravity well, the nukes for deep space sublight maneuverings, and the great stardrives themselves. The lights of his sled flickered past the encircling ring of nukes and sent long, bright streaks along the sides of the closed cylinders of the stardrives, the huge engines that bent the stuff of spacetime, encased in webs of metal and crystal.

At the end of the tunnel was a great circular door, reinforced metal, closed: the main airlock.

Christopheris set the sled down, dismounted— pulling his boots free of the sled's magnetic grip with an effort—and moved to the airlock. This was the hardest part, he thought. The headless body of Thale Lasamer was tethered loosely to a massive support strut by the lock, like a grisly guardian of the way. The xenobiologist had to stare at it while he waited for the lock to cycle. Whenever he glanced away, somehow he would find his eyes creeping back to it. The body looked almost natural, as if it had never had a head. Christopheris tried to remember what Lasamer had looked like, but the features would not come to mind. He moved uncomfortably, but then the lock door slid open and he gratefully entered the chamber to cycle through.

He was alone in the *Nightflyer*.

A cautious man, Christopheris kept his suit on, though he collapsed the helmet and yanked loose the suddenly limp metallic fabric so it fell behind his back like a hood. He could snap it in place quickly enough if the need arose. In cargo hold four, where they had stored their equipment, the xenobiologist found what he was looking for: a portable cutting laser, charged and ready. Low power, but it would do.

Slow and clumsy in weightlessness, he pulled himself down the corridor into the darkened lounge.

It was chilly inside, the air cold on his cheeks. He tried not to notice. He braced himself at the door and pushed off across the width of the room, sailing above the furniture, which was all safely bolted into place. As he drifted towards his objective, something wet and cold touched his face. It startled him, but it was gone before he could quite make out what it was.

When it happened again, Christopheris snatched at it, caught it, and felt briefly sick. He had forgotten. No one had cleaned the lounge yet. The—the *remains* were still there, floating now, blood and flesh and bits of bone and brain. All around him.

He reached the far wall, stopped himself with his arms, pulled himself down to where he wanted to go. The bulkhead. The wall. No doorway was visible, but the metal couldn't be very thick. Beyond was the control room, the computer access, safety, power. Rojan Christopheris did not think of himself as a vindictive man. He did not intend to harm Royd Eris, that judgment was not his to make. He would take control of the *Nightflyer,* warn Eris away, make certain the man stayed sealed in his suit. He would take them all back without any more mysteries, any more killings. The Academy arbiters could listen to the story, and probe Eris, and decide the right and wrong of it, guilt and innocence, what should be done.

The cutting laser emitted a thin pencil of scarlet

light. Christopheris smiled and applied it to the bulkhead. It was slow work, but he had patience. They would not have missed him, quiet as he'd been, and if they did they would assume he was off sledding after some hunk of salvage. Eris's repairs would take hours, maybe days, to finish. The bright blade of the laser smoked where it touched the metal. Christopheris applied himself diligently.

Something moved on the periphery of his vision, just a little flicker, barely seen. A floating bit of brain, he thought. A sliver of bone. A bloody piece of flesh, hair still hanging from it. Horrible things, but nothing to worry about. He was a biologist, he was used to blood and brains and flesh. And worse, and worse; he had dissected many an alien in his day, cutting through chitin and mucous, pulsing stinking food sacs and poisonous spines, he had seen and touched it all.

Again the motion caught his eye, teased at it. Not wanting to, Christopheris found himself drawn to look. He could not *not* look, somehow, just as he had been unable to ignore the headless corpse near the airlock. He looked.

It was an eye.

Christopheris trembled and the laser slipped sharply off to one side, so he had to wrestle with it to bring it back to the channel he was cutting. His heart raced. He tried to calm himself. Nothing to be frightened of. No one was home, and if Royd should return, well, he had the laser as a weapon and he had his suit on if an airlock blew.

He looked at the eye again, willing away his fear. It was just an eye, Thale Lasamer's eye, pale blue, bloody but intact, the same watery eye the boy had when alive, nothing supernatural. A piece of dead flesh, floating in the lounge amid other pieces of dead flesh. Someone should have cleaned up the lounge, Christopheris thought angrily. It was indecent to leave it like this, it was uncivilized.

The eye did not move. The other grisly bits were drifting on the air currents that flowed across the room, but the eye was still. It neither bobbed nor spun. It was fixed on him. Staring.

He cursed himself and concentrated on the laser, on his cutting. He had burned an almost straight line up the bulkhead for about a meter. He began another at a right angle.

The eye watched dispassionately. Christopheris suddenly found he could not stand it. One hand released its grip on the laser, reached out, caught the eye, flung it across the room. The action made him lose balance. He

tumbled backward, the laser slipping from his grasp, his arms flapping like the wings of some absurd heavy bird. Finally he caught an edge of the table and stopped himself.

The laser hung in the center of the room, floating amid coffeepots and pieces of human debris, still firing, turning slowly. That did not make sense. It should have ceased fire when he released it. A malfunction, Christopheris thought nervously. Smoke was rising where the thin line of the laser traced a path across the carpet.

With a shiver of fear, Christopheris realized that the laser was turning towards him.

He raised himself, put both hands flat against the table, pushed up out of the way, bobbing towards the ceiling.

The laser was turning more swiftly now.

He pushed away from the ceiling hard, slammed into a wall, grunted in pain, bounced off the floor, kicked. The laser was spinning quickly, chasing him. Christopheris soared, braced himself for another ricochet off the ceiling. The beam swung around, but not fast enough. He'd get it while it was still firing off in the other direction.

He moved close, reached, and saw the eye. It hung just above the laser. Staring.

Rojan Christopheris made a small whimpering sound low in his throat, and his hand hesitated—not long, but long enough—and the scarlet beam came up and around.

Its touch was a light, hot caress across his neck.

It was more than an hour later before they missed him. Karoly d'Branin noticed his absence first, called for him over the comm link, and got no answer. He discussed it with the others.

Royd Eris moved his sled back from the armor plate he had just mounted, and through his helmet Melantha Jhirl could see the lines around his mouth grow hard.

It was just then that the noises began.

A shrill bleat of pain and fear, followed by moans and sobbing. Terrible wet sounds, like a man choking on his own blood. They all heard. The sounds filled their helmets. And almost clear amid the anguish was something that sounded like a word: "Help."

"That's Christopheris," a woman's voice said. Lindran.

"He's hurt," Dannel added. "He's crying for help. Can't you hear it?"

"Where—?" someone started.

"The ship," Lindran said. "He must have returned to the ship."

Royd Eris said, "The fool. No. I warned—"

"We're going to check," Lindran announced. Dannel cut free the hull fragment they had been bringing in, and it spun away, tumbling. Their sled angled down towards the *Nightflyer*.

"Stop," Royd said. "I'll return to my chambers and check from there, if you wish, but you may not enter the ship. Stay outside until I give you clearance."

The terrible sounds went on and on.

"Go to hell," Lindran snapped at him over the open circuit.

Karoly d'Branin had his sled in motion, too, hastening after the linguists, but he had been farther out and it was a long way back to the ship. "Royd, what can you mean, we must help, don't you see? He is hurt, listen to him. Please, my friend."

"No," Royd said. "Karoly, stop! If Rojan went back to the ship alone, he is dead."

"How do you know that?" Dannel demanded. "Did you arrange it? Set traps in case we disobeyed you?"

"No," Royd said, "listen to me. You can't help him now. Only I could have helped him, and he did not listen to me. Trust me. Stop." His voice was despairing.

In the distance, d'Branin's sled slowed. The linguists did not. "We've already listened to you too damn much, I'd say," Lindran said. She almost had to shout to be heard above the noises, the whimpers and moans, the awful wet sucking sounds, the distorted pleas for help. Agony filled their universe. "Melantha," Lindran continued, "keep Eris right where he is. We'll go carefully, find out what is happening inside, but I don't want him getting back to his controls. Understood?"

Melantha Jhirl hesitated. The sounds beat against her ears. It was hard to think.

Royd swung his sled around to face her, and she could feel the weight of his stare. "Stop them," he said. "Melantha, Karoly, order it. They will not listen to me. They do not know what they are doing." He was clearly in pain.

In his face Melantha found decision. "Go back inside quickly, Royd. Do what you can. I'm going to try to intercept them."

"Whose side are you on?" Lindran demanded.

Royd nodded to her across the gulf, but Melantha was already in motion. Her sled backed clear of the work area, congested with hull fragments and other debris, then accelerated briskly as she raced around the exterior of the *Nightflyer* towards the driveroom.

But even as she approached, she knew it was too late. The linguists were too close, and already moving much faster than she was.

"Don't," she said, authority in her tone. "Christopheris is dead."

"His ghost is crying for help, then," Lindran replied. "When they tinkered you together, they must have damaged the genes for hearing, bitch."

"The ship isn't safe."

"Bitch," was all the answer she got.

Karoly's sled pursued vainly. "Friends, you must stop, please, I beg it of you. Let us talk this out together."

The sounds were his only reply.

"I am your superior," he said. "I order you to wait outside. Do you hear me? I order it, I invoke the authority of the Academy of Human Knowledge. Please, my friends, please."

Melantha watched helplessly as Lindran and Dannel vanished down the long tunnel of the driveroom.

A moment later she halted her own sled near the waiting black mouth, debating whether she should follow them on into the *Nightflyer*. She might be able to catch them before the airlock opened.

Royd's voice, hoarse counterpoint to the sounds, answered her unvoiced question. "Stay, Melantha. Proceed no farther."

She looked behind her. Royd's sled was approaching.

"What are you doing here? Royd, use your own lock. You have to get back inside!"

"Melantha," he said calmly, "I cannot. The ship will not respond to me. The lock will not dilate. The main lock in the driveroom is the only one with manual override. I am trapped outside. I don't want you or Karoly inside the ship until I can return to my console."

Melantha Jhirl looked down the shadowed barrel of the driveroom, where the linguists had vanished.

"What will—"

"Beg them to come back, Melantha. Plead with them. Perhaps there is still time."

She tried. Karoly d'Branin tried as well. The twisted symphony of pain and pleading went on and on, but they could not raise Dannel or Lindran at all.

"They've cut out their comm," Melantha said furiously. "They don't want to listen to us. Or that . . . that sound."

Royd's sled and d'Branin's reached her at the same time. "I do not understand," Karoly said. "Why can you not enter, Royd? What is happening?"

"It is simple, Karoly," Royd replied. "I am being kept outside until—until—"

"Yes?" prompted Melantha.

"—until Mother is done with them."

The linguists left their vacuum sled next to the one that Christopheris had abandoned, and cycled through the airlock in unseemly haste, with hardly a glance for the grim headless doorman.

Inside they paused briefly to collapse their helmets. "I can still hear him," Dannel said. The sounds were faint inside the ship.

Lindran nodded. "It's coming from the lounge. Hurry."

They kicked and pulled their way down the corridor in less than a minute. The sounds grew steadily louder, nearer. "He's in there," Lindran said when they reached the doorway.

"Yes," Dannel said, "but is he alone? We need a weapon. What if . . . Royd had to be lying. There is someone else on board. We need to defend ourselves."

Lindran would not wait. "There are two of us," she said. "Come *on*!" She launched herself through the doorway, calling Christopheris by name.

It was dark inside. What little light there was spilled through the door from the corridor. Her eyes took a long moment to adjust. Everything was confused; walls and ceilings and floor were all the same, she had no sense of direction. "Rojan," she called, dizzily. "Where are you?" The lounge seemed empty, but maybe it was only the light, or her sense of unease.

"Follow the sound," Dannel suggested. He hung in the door, peering warily about for a minute, and then began to feel his way cautiously down a wall, groping with his hands.

As if in response to his comment, the sobbing sounds grew suddenly louder. But they seemed to come first from one corner of the room, then from another.

Lindran, impatient, propelled herself across the chamber, searching. She brushed against a wall in the kitchen area, and that made her think of weapons, and Dannel's fears. She knew where the utensils were stored. "Here," she said a moment later, turning towards him. "Here, I've got a knife, that should thrill you." She flourished it, and brushed against a floating bubble of liquid as big as her fist. It burst and re-formed into a hundred smaller globules. One moved past her face, close, and she tasted it. Blood.

But Lasamer had been dead a long time. His blood ought to have dried by now, she thought.

"Oh, merciful god," said Dannel.

"What?" Lindran demanded. "Did you find him?"

Dannel was fumbling his way back towards the door, creeping along the wall like an oversized insect, back the way he had come. "Get out, Lindran," he warned. *"Hurry!"*

"Why?" She trembled despite herself. "What's wrong?"

"The screams," he said. "The wall, Lindran, the wall. The sounds."

"You're not making sense," she snapped. "Get ahold of yourself."

He gibbered, "Don't you see? The sounds are coming from the *wall*. The communicator. Faked. Simulated." Dannel reached the door, and dove through it, sighing audibly. He did not wait for her. He bolted down the corridor and was gone, pulling himself hand over hand wildly, his feet thrashing and kicking behind him.

Lindran braced herself and moved to follow.

The sounds came from in front of her, from the door. "Help me," it said, in Rojan Christopheris's voice. She heard moaning and that terrible wet choking sound, and she stopped.

From her side came a wheezing, ghastly, death rattle. "Ahhhh," it moaned, loudly, building in a counterpoint to the other noise. "Help me."

"Help me, help me, help me," said Christopheris from the darkness behind her.

Coughing and a weak groan sounded under her feet.

"Help me," all the voices chorused, "help me, help me, help me." Recordings, she thought, recordings being played back. "Help me, help me, help me, help me." All the voices rose higher and louder, and the words turned into a scream, and the scream ended in wet choking, in wheezes and gasps and death. Then the sounds stopped. Just like that; turned off.

Lindran kicked off, floated towards the door, knife in hand.

Something dark and silent crawled from beneath the dinner table and rose to block her path. She saw it clearly for a moment, as it emerged between her and the light. Rojan Christopheris, still in his vacuum suit, but with the helmet pulled off. He had something in his hand that he raised to point at her. It was a laser, Lindran saw, a simple cutting laser.

She was moving straight towards him, coasting, helpless. She flailed and tried to stop herself, but she could not.

When she got quite close, she saw that Rojan had a second mouth below his chin, a long blackened slash, and it was grinning at her, and little droplets of blood flew from it, wetly, as he moved.

Dannel rushed down the corridor in a frenzy of fear, bruising himself as he smashed off walls and doorways. Panic and weightlessness made him clumsy. He kept glancing over his shoulder as he fled, hoping to see Lindran coming after him, but terrified of what he might see in her stead. Every time he looked back, he lost his sense of balance and went tumbling again.

It took a long, *long* time for the airlock to open. As he waited, trembling, his pulse began to slow. The sounds had dwindled behind him, and there was no sign of pursuit. He steadied himself with an effort. Once inside the lock chamber, with the inner door sealed between him and the lounge, he began to feel safe.

Suddenly Dannel could barely remember why he had been so terrified.

And he was ashamed; he had run, abandoned Lindran. And for what? What had frightened him so? An empty lounge? Noises from the walls? A rational explanation for that forced itself on him all at once. It only meant that poor Christopheris was somewhere else in the ship, that's all, just somewhere else, alive and in pain, spilling his agony into a comm unit.

Dannel shook his head ruefully. He'd hear no end of this, he knew. Lindran liked to taunt him. She would never let him forget it. But at least he would return, and apologize. That would count for something. Resolute, he reached out and killed the cycle on the airlock, then reversed it. The air that had been partially sucked out came gusting back into the chamber.

As the inner door rolled back, Dannel felt his fear return briefly, an instant of stark terror when he wondered what might have emerged from the lounge to wait for him in the corridors of the *Nightflyer*. He faced the fear and willed it away. He felt strong.

When he stepped out, Lindran was waiting.

He could see neither anger nor disdain in her curiously calm features, but he pushed himself towards her and tried to frame a plea for forgiveness anyway. "I don't know why I—"

With languid grace, her hand came out from behind her back. The knife flashed up in a killing arc, and that was when Dannel finally noticed the hole burned in her suit, still smoking, just between her breasts.

"Your *mother*?" Melantha Jhirl said incredulously as they hung helpless in the emptiness beyond the ship.

"She can hear everything we say," Royd replied. "But at this point it no longer makes any difference. Rojan must have done something very foolish, very threatening. Now she is determined to kill you all."

"She, she, what do you mean?" D'Branin's voice was puzzled. "Royd, surely you do not tell us that your mother is still alive. You said she died even before you were born."

"She did, Karoly," Royd said. "I did not lie to you."

"No," Melantha said. "I didn't think so. But you did not tell us the whole truth either."

Royd nodded. "Mother is dead, but her—her spirit still lives, and animates my *Nightflyer*." He sighed. "Perhaps it would be more fitting to say her *Nightflyer*. My control has been tenuous at best."

"Royd," d'Branin said, "spirits do not exist. They are not real. There is no survival after death. My *volcryn* are more real than any ghosts."

"I don't believe in ghosts either," said Melantha curtly.

"Call it what you will, then," Royd said. "My term is as good as any. The reality is unchanged by the terminology. My mother, or some part of my mother, lives in the *Nightflyer,* and she is killing all of you as she has killed others before."

"Royd, you do not make sense," d'Branin said.

"Quiet, Karoly. Let the captain explain."

"Yes," Royd said. "The *Nightflyer* is very—very advanced, you know. Automated, self-repairing, large. It had to be, if Mother were to be freed from the necessity of a crew. It was built on Newholme, you will recall. I have never been there, but I understand that Newholme's technology is quite sophisticated. Avalon could not duplicate this ship, I suspect. There are few worlds that could."

"The point, captain?"

"The point—the point is the computers, Melantha. They had to be extraordinary. They are, believe me, they are. Crystal-matrix cores, lasergrid data retrieval, full sensory extension, and other—features."

"Are you trying to tell us that the *Nightflyer* is an Artificial Intelligence? Lommie Thorne suspected as much."

"She was wrong," Royd said. "My ship is not an Artificial Intelligence, not as I understand it. But it is something close. Mother had a capacity for personality impress built in. She filled the central crystal with her own memories, desires, quirks, her loves and her—her hates. That was why she could trust the computer with my education, you see? She knew it would raise me as she herself would, had she the patience. She programmed it in certain other ways as well."

"And you cannot deprogram, my friend?" Karoly asked.

Royd's voice was despairing. "I have *tried*, Karoly. But I am a weak hand at systems work, and the programs are very complicated, the machines very sophisticated. At least three times I have eradicated her, only to have her surface once again. She is a phantom program, and I cannot track her. She comes and goes as she will. A ghost, do you see? Her memories and her personality are so intertwined with the programs that run the *Nightflyer* that I cannot get rid of her without destroying the central crystal, wiping the entire system. But that would leave me helpless. I could never reprogram, and with the computers down the entire ship would fail, drivers, life support, everything. I would have to leave the *Nightflyer,* and that would kill me."

"You should have told us, my friend," Karoly d'Branin said. "On Avalon, we have many cyberneticists, some very great minds. We might have aided you. We could have provided expert help. Lommie Thorne might have helped you."

"Karoly, I have *had* expert help. Twice I have brought systems specialists on board. The first one told me what I have just told you; that it was impossible without wiping the programs completely. The second had trained on Newholme. She thought she might be able to help me. Mother killed her."

"You are still holding something back," Melantha Jhirl said. "I understand how your cybernetic ghost can open and close airlocks at will and arrange other accidents of that nature. But how do you explain what she did to Thale Lasamer?"

"Ultimately I must bear the guilt," Royd replied. "My loneliness led me to a grievous error. I thought I could safeguard you, even with a telepath among you. I have carried other riders safely. I watch them constantly, warn them away from dangerous acts. If Mother attempts to interfere, I countermand her directly from the master control console. That usually works. Not always. Usually. Before this trip she had killed only five times, and the first three died when I was quite young. That was how I learned about her, about her presence in my ship. That party included a telepath, too.

"I should have known better, Karoly. My hunger for life has doomed you all to death. I overestimated my own abilities, and underestimated her fear of exposure. She strikes out when she is threatened, and telepaths are always a threat. They sense her, you see. A malign, looming presence, they tell me, something cool and hostile and inhuman."

"Yes," Karoly d'Branin said, "yes, that was what Thale said. An alien, he was certain of it."

"No doubt she feels alien to a telepath used to the familiar contours of organic minds. Hers is not a human brain, after all. What it is I cannot say—a complex of crystallized memories, a hellish network of interlocking programs, a meld of circuitry and spirit. Yes, I can understand why she might feel alien."

"You still haven't explained how a computer program could explode a man's skull," Melantha said.

"You wear the answer between your breasts, Melantha."

"My whisperjewel?" she said, puzzled. She felt it then, beneath her vacuum suit and her clothing; a touch of cold, a vague hint of eroticism that made her shiver. It was as if his mention had been enough to make the gem come alive.

"I was not familiar with whisperjewels until you told me of yours," Royd said, "but the principle is the same. Esper-etched, you said. Then you know that psionic power can be stored. The central core of my computer is resonant crystal, many times larger than your tiny jewel. I think Mother impressed it as she lay dying."

"Only an esper can etch a whisperjewel," Melantha said.

"You never asked the *why* of it, either of you," Royd said. "You never asked why Mother hated people so. She was born gifted, you see. On Avalon she might have been a class one, tested and trained and honored, her talent nurtured and rewarded. I think she might have been very famous. She might have been stronger than a class one, but perhaps it is only after death that she acquired such power, linked as she is to the *Nightflyer*.

"The point is moot. She was not born on Avalon. On Vess, her ability was seen as a curse, something alien and fearful. So they cured her of it. They used drugs and electroshock and hypnotraining that made her violently ill whenever she tried to use her talent. They used other, less savory methods as well. She never lost her power, of course, only the ability to use it effectively, to control it with her conscious mind. It remained part of her, suppressed, erratic, a source of shame and pain, surfacing violently in times of great emotional stress. And half a decade of institutional care almost drove her insane. No wonder she hated people."

"What was her talent? Telepathy?"

"No. Oh, some rudimentary ability perhaps. I have read that all psi talents have several latent abilities in addition to their one developed strength. But Mother could not read minds. She had some empathy, although her cure had twisted it curiously, so that the emotions she felt literally sickened her. But her major strength, the talent they took five years to shatter and destroy, was teke."

Melantha Jhirl swore. "Of *course* she hated gravity! Telekinesis under weightlessness is—"

"Yes," Royd finished. "Keeping the *Nightflyer* under gravity tortures me, but it limits Mother."

In the silence that followed that comment, each of them looked down the dark cylinder of the driveroom. Karoly d'Branin moved awkwardly on his sled. "Dannel and Lindran have not returned," he said.

"They are probably dead," Royd said dispassionately.

"What will we do, then? We must plan. We cannot wait here indefinitely."

"The first question is what *I* can do," Royd Eris replied. "I have talked freely, you'll note. You deserved to know. We have passed the point where ignorance was a protection. Obviously things have gone too far. There have been too many deaths and you have been witness to all of them. Mother cannot allow you to return to Avalon alive."

"True," said Melantha. "But what shall she do with you? Is your own status in doubt, captain?"

"The crux of the problem," Royd admitted. "You are still three moves ahead, Melantha. I wonder if it will suffice. Your opponent is four ahead in this game, and most of your pawns are already captured. I fear checkmate is imminent."

"Unless I can persuade my opponent's king to desert, no?"

She could see Royd's wan smile. "She would probably kill me too if I choose to side with you. She does not need me."

Karoly d'Branin was slow to grasp the point. "But—but what else could—"

"My sled has a laser. Yours do not. I could kill you both, right now, and thereby earn my way back into the *Nightflyer*'s good graces."

Across the three meters that lay between their sleds,

Melantha's eyes met Royd's. Her hands rested easily on the thruster controls. "You could try, captain. Remember, the improved model isn't easy to kill."

"I would not kill you, Melantha Jhirl," Royd said seriously. "I have lived sixty-eight standard years and I have never lived at all. I am tired, and you tell grand, gorgeous lies. Will you really touch me?"

"Yes."

"I risk a lot for that touch. Yet in a way it is no risk at all. If we lose, we will all die together. If we win, well, I shall die anyway when they destroy the *Nightflyer,* either that or live as a freak in an orbital hospital, and I would prefer death."

"We will build you a new ship, captain," Melantha promised.

"Liar," Royd replied. But his tone was cheerful. "No matter. I have not had much of a life anyway. Death does not frighten me. If we win, you must tell me about your *volcryn* once again, Karoly. And you, Melantha, you must play chess with me, and find a way to touch me, and . . ."

"And sex with you?" she finished, smiling.

"If you would," he said quietly. He shrugged. "Well, Mother has heard all of this. Doubtless she will listen carefully to any plans we might make, so there is no sense making them. Now there is no chance that the control lock will admit me, since it is keyed directly into the ship's computer. So we must follow the others through the driveroom, and enter through the main lock, and take what small chances we are given. If I can reach my console and restore gravity, perhaps we can win. If not—"

He was interrupted by a low groan.

For an instant Melantha thought the *Nightflyer* was wailing at them again, and she was surprised that it was so stupid as to try the same tactic twice. Then the groan sounded once more, and in the back of Karoly d'Branin's sled, the forgotten fourth member of their company struggled against the bonds that held her down. D'Branin hastened to free her, and Agatha Marij-Black tried to rise to her feet and almost floated off the sled, until he caught her hand and pulled her back. "Are you well?" he asked. "Can you hear me? Have you pain?"

Imprisoned beneath a transparent faceplate, wide, frightened eyes flicked rapidly from Karoly to Melantha to Royd, and then to the broken *Nightflyer*. Melantha wondered whether the woman was insane, and started to caution d'Branin, when Marij-Black spoke.

"The *volcryn*!" was all she said. "Oh. The *volcryn*!"

Around the mouth of the driveroom, the ring of nuclear engines took on a faint glow. Melantha Jhirl heard Royd suck in his breath sharply. She gave the thruster controls of her sled a violent twist. "Hurry," she said loudly. "The *Nightflyer* is preparing to move."

A third of the way down the long barrel of the drive-room, Royd pulled abreast of her, stiff and menacing in his black, bulky armor. Side by side they sailed past the cylindrical stardrives and the cyberwebs; ahead, dimly lit, was the main airlock and its ghastly sentinel.

"When we reach the lock, jump over to my sled," Royd said. "I want to stay armed and mounted, and the chamber is not large enough for two sleds."

Melantha Jhirl risked a quick glance behind her. "Karoly," she called. "Where are you?"

"Outside, my love, my friend," the answer came. "I cannot come. Forgive me."

"We have to stay together!"

"No," d'Branin said, "no, I could not risk it, not when we are so close. It would be so tragic, so futile, Melantha. To come so close and fail. Death I do not mind, but I must see them first, finally, after all these years."

"My mother is going to move the ship," Royd cut in. "Karoly, you will be left behind, lost."

"I will wait," d'Branin replied. "My *volcryn* come, and I must wait for them."

Then the time for conversation was gone, for the air-lock was almost upon them. Both sleds slowed and stopped, and Royd Eris reached out and began the cycle while Melantha Jhirl moved to the rear of his huge oval worksled. When the outer door moved aside, they glided through into the lock chamber.

"When the inner door opens it will begin," Royd told her evenly. "The permanent furnishings are either built-in or welded or bolted into place, but the things that your team brought on board are not. Mother will use those things as weapons. And beware of doors, airlocks, any equipment tied into the *Nightflyer*'s computer. Need I warn you not to unseal your suit?"

"Hardly," she replied.

Royd lowered the sled a little, and its grapplers made a metallic sound as they touched against the floor of the chamber.

The inner door hissed open, and Royd applied his thrusters.

Inside, Dannel and Lindran waited, swimming in a haze of blood. Dannel had been slit from crotch to throat and his intestines moved like a nest of pale, angry snakes. Lindran still held the knife. They swam closer, moving with a grace they had never possessed in life.

Royd lifted his foremost grapplers and smashed them to the side as he surged forward. Dannel caromed off a bulkhead, leaving a wide wet mark where he struck, and more of his guts came sliding out. Lindran lost control of the knife. Royd accelerated past them, driving up the corridor through the cloud of blood.

"I'll watch behind," Melantha said. She turned and put her back to his. Already the two corpses were safely behind them. The knife was floating uselessly in the air. She started to tell Royd that they were all right, when the blade abruptly shifted and came after them, gripped by some invisible force.

"Swerve!" she cried.

The sled shot wildly to one side. The knife missed by a full meter, and glanced ringingly off a bulkhead.

But it did not drop. It came at them again.

The lounge loomed ahead. Dark.

"The door is too narrow," Royd said. "We will have to abandon—" As he spoke, they hit; he wedged the sled squarely into the doorframe, and the sudden impact jarred them loose.

For a moment Melantha floated clumsily in the corridor, her head whirling, trying to sort up from down. The knife slashed at her, opening her suit and her shoulder clear through to the bone. She felt sharp pain and the warm flush of bleeding. "Damn," she shrieked. The knife came around again, spraying droplets of blood.

Melantha's hand darted out and caught it.

She muttered something under her breath and wrenched the blade free of the hand that had been gripping it.

Royd had regained the controls of his sled and seemed intent on some manipulation. Beyond him, in the dimness of the lounge, Melantha glimpsed a dark semi-human form rise into view.

"Royd!" she warned. The thing activated its small laser. The pencil beam caught Royd square in the chest.

He touched his own firing stud. The sled's heavy-duty laser came alive, a shaft of sudden brilliance. It cindered Christopheris' weapon and burned off his right arm and part of his chest. The beam hung in the air, throbbing, and smoked against the far bulkhead.

Royd made some adjustments and began cutting a hole. "We'll be through in five minutes or less," he said curtly.

"Are you all right?" Melantha asked.

"I'm uninjured," he replied. "My suit is better armored than yours, and his laser was a low-powered toy."

Melantha turned her attention back to the corridor.

The linguists were pulling themselves towards her, one on each side of the passage, to come at her from two directions at once. She flexed her muscles. Her shoulder stabbed and screamed. Otherwise she felt strong, almost reckless. "The corpses are coming after us again," she told Royd. "I'm going to take them."

"Is that wise?" he asked. "There are two of them."

"I'm an improved model," Melantha said, "and they're dead." She kicked herself free of the sled and sailed towards Dannel in a high, graceful trajectory. He raised his hands to block her. She slapped them aside, bent one arm back and heard it snap, and drove her knife deep into his throat before she realized what a useless gesture that was. Blood oozed from his neck in a spreading cloud, but he continued to flail at her. His teeth snapped grotesquely.

Melantha withdrew her blade, seized him, and with all her considerable strength threw him bodily down the corridor. He tumbled, spinning wildly, and vanished into the haze of his own blood.

Melantha flew in the opposite direction, revolving lazily.

Lindran's hands caught her from behind.

Nails scrabbled against her faceplate until they began to bleed, leaving red streaks on the plastic.

Melantha whirled to face her attacker, grabbed a thrashing arm, and flung the woman down the passageway to crash into her struggling companion. The reaction sent her spinning like a top. She spread her arms and stopped herself, dizzy, gulping.

"I'm through," Royd announced.

Melantha turned to see. A smoking meter-square opening had been cut through one wall of the lounge. Royd killed the laser, gripped both sides of the doorframe, and pushed himself towards it.

A piercing blast of sound drilled through her head. She doubled over in agony. Her tongue flicked out and clicked off the comm; then there was blessed silence.

In the lounge it was raining. Kitchen utensils, glasses and plates, pieces of human bodies all lashed violently across the room, and glanced harmlessly off Royd's armored form. Melantha—eager to follow—drew back helplessly. That rain of death would cut her to pieces in her lighter, thinner vacuum suit. Royd reached the far wall and vanished into the secret control section of the ship. She was alone.

The *Nightflyer* lurched, and sudden acceleration provided a brief semblance of gravity. Melantha was thrown to one side. Her injured shoulder smashed painfully against the sled.

All up and down the corridor doors were opening.

Dannel and Lindran were moving towards her once again.

The *Nightflyer* was a distant star sparked by its nuclear engines. Blackness and cold enveloped them, and below was the unending emptiness of the Tempter's Veil, but Karoly d'Branin did not feel afraid. He felt strangely transformed.

The void was alive with promise.

"They *are* coming," he whispered. "Even I, who have no psi at all, even I can feel it. The Crey story must be so, even from light-years off they can be sensed. Marvelous!"

Agatha Marij-Black seemed small and shrunken. "The *volcryn,*" she muttered. "What good can they do us. I hurt. The ship is gone. D'Branin, my head aches." She made a small, frightened noise. "Thale said that, just after I injected him, before—before—you know. He said that his head hurt. It aches so terribly."

"Quiet, Agatha. Do not be afraid. I am here with you.

Wait. Think only of what we shall witness, think only of that!"

"I can sense them," the psipsych said.

D'Branin was eager. "Tell me, then. We have our little sled. We shall go to them. Direct me."

"Yes," she agreed. "Yes. Oh, yes."

Gravity returned; in a flicker, the universe became almost normal.

Melantha fell to the deck, landed easily and rolled, and was on her feet cat-quick.

The objects that had been floating ominously through the open doors along the corridor all came clattering down.

The blood was transformed from a fine mist to a slick covering on the corridor floor.

The two corpses dropped heavily from the air, and lay still.

Royd spoke to her from the communicators built into the walls. "I made it," he said.

"I noticed," she replied.

"I'm at the main control console. I have restored the gravity with a manual override, and I'm cutting off as many computer functions as possible. We're still not

safe, though. Mother will try to find a way around me. I'm countermanding her by sheer force, as it were. I cannot afford to overlook anything, and if my attention should lapse, even for a moment . . . Melantha, was your suit breached?"

"Yes. Cut at the shoulder."

"Change into another one. *Immediately.* I think the counterprogramming I'm doing will keep the locks sealed, but I can't take any chances."

Melantha was already running down the corridor, towards the cargo hold where the suits and equipment were stored.

"When you have changed," Royd continued, "dump the corpses into the mass conversion unit. You'll find the appropriate hatch near the driveroom airlock, just to the left of the lock controls. Convert any other loose objects that are not indispensable as well; scientific instruments, books, tapes, tableware—"

"Knives," suggested Melantha.

"By all means."

"Is teke still a threat, captain?"

"Mother is vastly weaker in a gravity field," Royd said. "She has to fight it. Even boosted by the *Nightflyer*'s power, she can only move one object at a time, and she has only a fraction of the lifting force she wields under weightless conditions. But the power is still there, remember. Also, it is possible she will find a way to circumvent me and cut out the gravity again. From here I can restore it in an instant, but I don't want any likely weapons lying around even for that brief period of time."

Melantha reached the cargo area. She stripped off her vacuum suit and slipped into another one in record time, wincing at the pain in her shoulder. It was bleeding badly, but she had to ignore it. She gathered up the discarded suit and a double armful of instruments and dumped them into the conversion chamber. Afterwards she turned her attention to the bodies. Dannel was no problem. Lindran crawled down the corridor after her as Melantha pushed him through, and thrashed weakly when it was her own turn, a grim reminder that the *Nightflyer*'s powers were not all gone. Melantha easily overcame Lindran's feeble struggles and forced her through.

Christopheris's burned, ruined body writhed in her grasp and snapped its teeth at her, but Melantha had no real trouble with it. While she was cleaning out the lounge, a kitchen knife came spinning at her head. It came slowly, though, and Melantha just batted it aside, then picked it up and added it to the pile for conversion. She was working through the cabins, carrying Agatha

Marij-Black's abandoned drugs and injection gun under her arm, when she heard Royd cry out.

A moment later a force like a giant invisible hand wrapped itself around her chest and squeezed and pulled her, struggling, to the floor.

Something was moving across the stars.

Dimly and far off, d'Branin could see it, though he could not yet make out details. But it was there, that was unmistakable, some vast shape that blocked off a section of the starscape. It was coming at them dead on.

How he wished he had his team with him now, his computer, his telepath, his experts, his instruments.

He pressed harder on the thrusters, and rushed to meet his *volcryn.*

Pinned to the floor, hurting, Melantha Jhirl risked opening her suit's comm. She had to talk to Royd. "Are you there?" she asked. "What's happen . . . happening?" The pressure was awful, and it was growing steadily worse.

She could barely move.

The answer was pained and slow in coming. ". . . outwitted . . . me," Royd's voice managed. ". . . hurts to . . . talk."

"Royd—"

". . . she . . . teked . . . the . . . dial . . . up . . . two . . . gees . . . three . . . higher . . . right . . . on . . . the . . . board . . . all . . . I . . . have to . . . to do . . . turn it . . . back . . . back . . . let me."

Silence. Then, finally, when Melantha was near despair, Royd's voice again. One word:

". . . can't . . ."

Melantha's chest felt as if it were supporting ten times her own weight. She could imagine the agony Royd must be in; Royd, for whom even one gravity was painful and dangerous. Even if the dial was an arm's length away, she knew his feeble musculature would never let him reach it. "Why," she started. Talking was not as hard for her as it seemed to be for him. "Why would . . . she turn *up* the . . . the gravity . . . it . . . weakens her, too . . . yes?"

". . . yes . . . but . . . in a . . . a time . . . hour . . . minute . . . my . . . my heart . . . will burst . . . and . . . and then . . . you alone . . . she . . . will . . . kill gravity . . . kill you. . . ."

Painfully Melantha reached out her arm and dragged

herself half a length down the corridor. "Royd . . . hold on . . . I'm coming. . . ." She dragged herself forward again. Agatha's drug kit was still under her arm, impossibly heavy. She eased it down and started to shove it aside. It felt as if it weighed a hundred kilos. She reconsidered. Instead she opened its lid.

The ampules were all neatly labeled. She glanced over them quickly, searching for adrenaline or synthastim, anything that might give her the strength she needed to reach Royd. She found several stimulants, selected the strongest, and was loading it into the injection gun with awkward, agonized slowness when her eyes chanced on the supply of esperon.

Melantha did not know why she hesitated. Esperon was only one of a half-dozen psionic drugs in the kit, none of which could do her any good, but something about seeing it bothered her, reminded her of something she could not quite lay her finger on. She was trying to sort it out when she heard the noise.

"Royd," she said, "your mother . . . could she move . . . she couldn't move anything . . . teke it . . . in this high a gravity . . . could she?"

"Maybe," he answered, ". . . if . . . concentrate . . . all her . . . power . . . hard . . . may be possible . . . why?"

"Because," Melantha Jhirl said grimly, "because something . . . some*one* . . . is cycling through the airlock."

"It is not truly a ship, not as I thought it would be," Karoly d'Branin was saying. His suit, Academy-designed, had a built-in encoding device, and he was recording his comments for posterity, strangely secure in the certainty of his impending death. "The scale of it is difficult to imagine, difficult to estimate. Vast, vast. I have nothing but my wrist computer, no instruments, I cannot make accurate measurements, but I would say, oh, a hundred kilometers, perhaps as much as three hundred, across. Not solid mass, of course, not at all. It is delicate, airy, no ship as we know ships, no city either. It is—oh, beautiful—it is crystal and gossamer, alive with its own dim lights, a vast intricate kind of spider-webby craft—it reminds me a bit of the old starsail ships they used once, in the days before drive, but this great construct, it is not solid, it cannot be driven by light. It is no ship at all, really. It is all open to vacuum, it has no sealed cabins or life-support spheres, none visible to me, unless blocked from my line of sight in some fashion, and no, I cannot believe that, it is too open, too fragile. It moves quite rapidly. I would wish for the instrumentation to measure its speed, but it is enough to be here. I am taking the sled at right angles to it, to get clear of its path, but I cannot say that I will make it. It moves so much faster than we. Not at light speed, no, far below light speed, but still faster than the *Nightflyer* and its nuclear engines, I would guess . . . only a guess.

"The *volcryn* craft has no visible means of propulsion. In fact, I wonder how—perhaps it is a light-sail, laser-launched millennia ago, now torn and rotted by some unimaginable catastrophe—but no, it is too symmetrical, too beautiful, the webbings, the great shimmering veils near the nexus, the beauty of it.

"I must describe it, I must be more accurate, I know. It is difficult, I grow too excited. It is large, as I have said, kilometers across. Roughly—let me count—yes, roughly octagonal in shape. The nexus, the center, is a bright area, a small darkness surrounded by a much greater area of light, but only the dark portion seems entirely solid—the lighted areas are translucent, I can see stars through them, though discolored, shifted towards the purple. Veils, I call those the veils. From the nexus and the veils, eight long—oh, vastly long—spurs project, not quite spaced evenly, so it is not a true geometric octagon—ah, I see better now, one of the spurs is shifting, oh, very slowly, the veils are rippling—they are mobile, then, those projections, and the webbing runs from one spur to the next, around and around, but there are—patterns, odd patterns, it is not at all the simple webbing of a spider. I cannot quite see order in the patterns, in the traceries of the webs, but I feel sure the order is there, the meaning is waiting to be found.

"There are lights. Have I mentioned the lights? The lights are brightest around the center nexus, but they are nowhere very bright, a dim violet. Some visible radiation, then, but not much. I would like to take an ultraviolet reading of this craft, but I do not have the instrumentation. The lights move. The veils seem to ripple, and lights run constantly up and down the length of the spurs, at differing rates of speed, and sometimes other lights can be seen transversing the webbing, moving across the patterns. I do not know what the lights are. Some form of communication, perhaps. I cannot tell whether they emanate from inside the craft or outside. I—oh! There was another light just then. Between the spurs, a brief flash, a starburst. It is gone now, already. It was more intense than the others, indigo. I feel so helpless, so ignorant. But they are beautiful, my *volcryn*. . . .

"The myths, they—this is really not much like the legends, not truly. The size, the lights. The *volcryn* have

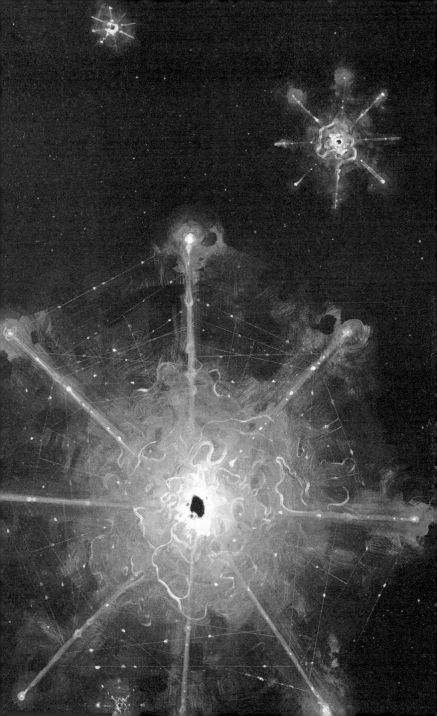

often been linked to lights, but those reports were so vague, they might have meant anything, described anything from a laser propulsion system to simple exterior lighting. I could not know it meant this. Ah, what mystery! The ship is still too far away to see the finer detail. It is so large, I do not think we shall get clear of it. It seems to have turned towards us, I think, yet I may be mistaken, it is only an impression. My instruments, if I only had my instruments. Perhaps the darker area in the center is a craft, a life capsule. The *volcryn* must be inside it. I wish my team were with me, and Thale, poor Thale. He was a class one, we might have made contact, might have communicated with them. The things we would learn! The things they have seen! To think how old this craft is, how ancient the race, how long they have been outbound . . . it fills me with awe. Communication would be such a gift, such an impossible gift, but they are so alien."

"*D'Branin,*" Agatha Marij-Black said in a low, urgent voice. "Can't you feel?"

Karoly d'Branin looked at her as if seeing her for the first time.

"Can *you* feel them? You are a three, can you sense them now, strongly?"

"Long ago," the psipsych said, "long ago."

"Can you project? Talk to them, Agatha. Where are they? In the center area? The dark?"

"Yes," she replied, and she laughed. Her laugh was shrill and hysterical, and d'Branin had to recall that she was a very sick woman. "Yes, in the center, d'Branin, that's where the pulses come from. Only you're wrong about them. It's not a them at all, your legends are all lies, lies, I wouldn't be surprised if we were the first ever to see your *volcryn,* to come this close. The others, those aliens of yours, they merely *felt,* deep and distantly, sensed a bit of the nature of the *volcryn* in their dreams and visions, and fashioned the rest to suit themselves. Ships, and wars, and a race of eternal travelers, it is all—all—"

"Yes. What do you mean, Agatha, my friend? You do not make sense. I do not understand."

"No," Marij-Black said, "you do not, do you?" Her voice was suddenly gentle. "You cannot feel it, as I can. So clear now. This must be how a one feels, all the time. A one full of esperon."

"What do you feel? *What?*"

"It's not a *them,* Karoly. It's an *it.* Alive, Karoly, and quite mindless, I assure you."

"Mindless?" d'Branin said. "No, you must be wrong, you are not reading correctly. I will accept that it is a single creature if you say so, a single great marvelous star-traveler, but how can it be mindless? You sensed it, its mind, its telepathic emanations. You and the whole of the Crey sensitives and all the others. Perhaps its thoughts are too alien for you to read."

"Perhaps. But what I do read is not so terribly alien at all. Only animal. Its thoughts are slow and dark and strange, hardly thoughts at all, faint. Stirrings cold and distant. The brain must be huge all right, I grant you that, but it can't be devoted to conscious thought."

"What do you mean?"

"The propulsion system, d'Branin. Don't you *feel*? The pulses? They are threatening to rip off the top of my skull. Can't you guess what is driving your damned *volcryn* across the galaxy? And why they avoid gravity wells? Can't you guess how it is moving?"

"No," d'Branin said, but even as he denied it a dawn of comprehension broke across his face, and he looked away from his companion, back at the swelling immensity of the *volcryn,* its lights moving, its veils a-ripple as it came on and on, across light-years, light-centuries, across eons.

When he looked back at her, he mouthed only a single word: "Teke," he said.

She nodded.

* * *

Melantha Jhirl struggled to lift the injection gun and press it against an artery. It gave a single loud hiss, and the drug flooded her system. She lay back and gathered her strength and tried to think. Esperon, esperon, why was that important? It had killed Lasamer, made him a victim of his own latent abilities, multiplied his power and his vulnerability. Psi. It all came back to psi.

The inner door of the airlock opened. The headless corpse came through.

It moved with jerks, unnatural shufflings, never lifting its legs from the floor. It sagged as it moved, half crushed by the weight upon it. Each shuffle was crude and sudden; some grim force was literally yanking one leg forward, then the next. It moved in slow motion, arms stiff by its sides.

But it moved.

Melantha summoned her own reserves and began to squirm away from it, never taking her eyes off its advance.

Her thoughts went round and round, searching for the piece out of place, the solution to the chess problem, finding nothing.

The corpse was moving faster than she was. Clearly, visibly, it was gaining.

Melantha tried to stand. She got to her knees with a grunt, her heart pounding. Then one knee. She tried to force herself up, to lift the impossible burden on her shoulders as if she were lifting weights. She was strong, she told herself. She was the improved model.

But when she put all her weight on one leg, her muscles would not hold her. She collapsed, awkwardly, and when she smashed against the floor it was as if she had fallen from a building. She heard a sharp *snap,* and a stab of agony flashed up her arm, her good arm, the arm she had tried to use to break her fall. The pain in her shoulder was terrible and intense. She blinked back tears and choked on her own scream.

The corpse was halfway up the corridor. It must be walking on two broken legs, she realized. It didn't care. A force greater than tendons and bone and muscle was holding it up.

"Melantha . . . heard you . . . are . . . you . . . Melantha?"

"Quiet," she snarled at Royd. She had no breath to waste on talk.

Now she used all the disciplines she had ever learned, willed away the pain. She kicked feebly, her boots scraping for purchase, and she pulled herself forward with her unbroken arm, ignoring the fire in her shoulder.

The corpse came on and on.

She dragged herself across the threshold of the lounge, worming her way under the crashed sled, hoping it would delay the cadaver. The thing that had been Thale Lasamer was a meter behind her.

In the darkness, in the lounge, where it had all begun, Melantha Jhirl ran out of strength.

Her body shuddered and she collapsed on the damp carpet, and she knew that she could go no farther.

On the far side of the door, the corpse stood stiffly. The sled began to shake. Then, with the scrape of metal against metal, it slid backward, moving in tiny sudden increments, jerking itself free and out of the way.

Psi. Melantha wanted to curse it, and cry. Vainly she wished for a psi power of her own, a weapon to blast apart the teke-driven corpse that stalked her. She was improved, she thought despairingly, but not improved enough. Her parents had given her all the genetic gifts they could arrange, but psi was beyond them. The genes were astronomically rare, recessive, and—

—and suddenly it came to her.

"Royd," she said, putting all of her remaining will into her words. She was weeping, wet, frightened. "The dial . . . *teke it.* Royd, teke it!"

His reply was faint, troubled. "... can't ... I don't ... Mother ... only ... her ... not me ... no ... Mother ..."

"Not Mother," she said, desperate. "You always ... say ... *Mother.* I forgot ... forgot. Not your mother ... listen ... you're a *clone* ... same genes ... you have it too ... power."

"Don't," he said. "Never ... must be ... sex-linked."

"No! It *isn't.* I know ... Promethean, Royd ... don't tell a Promethean ... about genes ... turn it!"

The sled jumped a third of a meter, and listed to the side. A path was clear.

The corpse came forward.

"... trying," Royd said. "Nothing ... I *can't!*"

"She *cured* you," Melantha said bitterly. "Better than ... she ... was cured ... prenatal ... but it's only ... suppressed ... you *can!*"

"I ... don't ... know ... how."

The corpse stood above her. Stopped. Its pale-fleshed hands trembled, spasmed, jerked upward. Long painted fingernails. Made claws. Began to rise.

Melantha swore. *"Royd!"*

"... sorry ..."

She wept and shook and made a futile fist.

And all at once the gravity was gone. Far, far away, she heard Royd cry out and then fall silent.

"The flashes come more frequently now," Karoly d'Branin dictated, "or perhaps it is simply that I am closer, that I can see them better. Bursts of indigo and deep violet, short and fast-fading. Between the webbing. A field, I think. The flashes are particles of hydrogen, the thin ethereal stuff of the reaches between the stars. They touch the field, between the webbing, the spurs, and shortly flare into the range of visible light. Matter to energy, yes, that is what I guess. My *volcryn* feeds.

"It fills half the universe, comes on and on. We shall not escape it, oh, so sad. Agatha is gone, silent, blood on her faceplate. I can almost see the dark area, almost, almost. I have a strange vision, in the center is a face, small, ratlike, without mouth or nose or eyes, yet still a face somehow, and it stares at me. The veils move so sensuously. The webbing looms around us.

"Ah, the light, the light!"

* * *

The corpse bobbed awkwardly into the air, its hands hanging limply before it. Melantha, reeling in the weightlessness, was suddenly violently sick. She ripped off the helmet, collapsed it, and pushed away from her own nausea, trying to ready herself for the *Nightflyer*'s furious assault.

But the body of Thale Lasamer floated dead and still, and nothing else moved in the darkened lounge. Finally Melantha recovered, and she moved to the corpse, weakly, and pushed it, a small and tentative shove. It sailed across the room.

"Royd?" she said uncertainly. There was no answer.

She pulled herself through the hole into the control chamber.

And found Royd Eris suspended in his armored suit. She shook him, but he did not stir. Trembling, Melantha Jhirl studied his suit, and then began to dismantle it. She touched him. "Royd," she said, "here. Feel, Royd, here, I'm here, feel it." His suit came apart easily, and she flung the pieces of it away. "Royd, *Royd.*"

Dead. Dead. His heart had given out. She punched it, pummeled it, tried to pound it into new life. It did not beat. Dead. Dead.

Melantha Jhirl moved back from him, blinded by her own tears, edged into the console, glanced down.

Dead. Dead.

But the dial on the gravity grid was set on zero. "Melantha," said a mellow voice from the walls.

I have held the *Nightflyer*'s crystalline soul within my hands.

It is deep red and multifaceted, large as my head, and icy to the touch. In its scarlet depths, two small sparks of smoky light burn fiercely, and sometimes seem to whirl.

I have crawled through the consoles, wound my way carefully past safeguards and cybernets, taking care to damage nothing, and I have laid rough hands on that great crystal, knowing it is where *she* lives.

And I cannot bring myself to wipe it. Royd's ghost has asked me not to.

Last night we talked about it once again, over brandy and chess in the lounge. Royd cannot drink, of course, but he sends his spectre to smile at me, and he tells me where he wants his pieces moved.

For the thousandth time he offered to take me back to Avalon, or any world of my choice, if only I would go outside and complete the repairs we abandoned so many years ago, so the *Nightflyer* might safely slip into stardrive.

For the thousandth time I refused.

He is stronger now, no doubt. Their genes are the same, after all. Their power is the same. Dying, he too found the strength to impress himself upon the great crystal. The ship is alive with both of them, and frequently they fight. Sometimes she outwits him for a moment, and the *Nightflyer* does odd, erratic things. The gravity goes up or down or off completely. Blankets wrap themselves around my throat when I sleep. Objects come hurtling out of dark corners.

Those times have come less frequently of late, though. When they do come, Royd stops her, or I do. Together, the *Nightflyer* is ours.

Royd claims he is strong enough alone, that he does not really need me, that he can keep her under check. I wonder. Over the chessboard, I still beat him nine games out of ten.

And there are other considerations. Our work, for one. Karoly would be proud of us. The *volcryn* will soon enter the mists of the Tempter's Veil, and we follow close behind. Studying, recording, doing all that old d'Branin would have wanted us to do. It is all in the computer, and on tape and paper as well, should the system ever be wiped. It will be interesting to see how the *volcryn* thrives in the Veil. Matter is so thick there, compared to the thin diet of interstellar hydrogen on which the creature has fed so many endless eons.

We have tried to communicate with it, with no success. I do not believe it is sentient at all. And lately Royd has tried to imitate its ways, gathering all his energies in an attempt to move the *Nightflyer* by teke. Sometimes, oddly, his mother even joins with him in those efforts. So far they have always failed, but we will keep trying.

So goes our work. We know our results will reach humanity. Royd and I have discussed it, and we have a plan. Before I die, when my time is near, I will destroy the central crystal and clear the computers, and afterwards I will set course manually for the close vicinity of an inhabited world. The *Nightflyer* will become a true ghost ship then. It will work. I have all the time I need, and I am an improved model.

I will not consider the other option, although it means much to me that Royd suggests it again and again. No doubt I could finish the repairs, and perhaps Royd could control the ship without me, and go on with the work. But that is not important.

I was wrong so many times. The esperon, the monitors, my control of the others; all of them my failures, payment for my hubris. Failure hurts. When I finally touched him, for the first and last and only time, his body was still warm. But he was gone already. He never felt my touch. I could not keep that promise.

But I can keep my other.

I will not leave him alone with her.

Ever.

ABOUT THE AUTHOR

GEORGE R. R. MARTIN is the #1 *New York Times* bestselling author of many novels, including the acclaimed series A Song of Ice and Fire—*A Game of Thrones, A Clash of Kings, A Storm of Swords, A Feast for Crows,* and *A Dance with Dragons*—as well as *Tuf Voyaging, Fevre Dream, The Armageddon Rag, Dying of the Light, Windhaven* (with Lisa Tuttle), and *Dreamsongs Volumes I* and *II*. He is also the creator of *The Lands of Ice and Fire,* a collection of maps from A Song of Ice and Fire featuring original artwork from illustrator and cartographer Jonathan Roberts, and *The World of Ice & Fire* (with Elio M. García, Jr., and Linda Antonsson). As a writer-producer, Martin has worked on *The Twilight Zone, Beauty and the Beast,* and various feature films and pilots that were never made. He lives with the lovely Parris in Santa Fe, New Mexico.

georgerrmartin.com
Facebook.com/GeorgeRRMartinofficial
Twitter: @GRRMSpeaking

ABOUT THE ILLUSTRATOR

DAVID PALUMBO is a Philadelphia-based painter known primarily for fantasy and horror genre illustration. His work is characterized by dark themes and moody atmosphere with a traditional painterly technique. Palumbo, a graduate of the Pennsylvania Academy of Fine Art, began his career showing in galleries in 2003, but his primary focus has long been centered on illustration. His images have since won numerous honors and have been featured in exhibits from New York to Paris.

dvpalumbo.com
Facebook.com/dvpalumbo
Instagram: @dvpalumbo